Death of Inn
Mrs Capper's C
David W Ro

© David W Robinson 2023

Edited by Maureen Vincent-Northam
Cover Design Rhys Vincent-Northam

Prologue

Good afternoon and welcome to Christine Capper's Comings and Goings, your weekly video blog of what's been happening in Haxford, brought to you this week by Felicia's Fantastic Fashions. Call Felicia if you want your say at the beginning of May.

Anger, disappointment, confusion. Those were the three dominant emotions after the joint affairs at Gaven Hall (which put a bit of a damper on memories of my niece's wonderful wedding) and at Allbrook Farm here in Haxford. It was all made worse by Eric Reitman's continued insistence that Christine Capper's Mystery Hour had to change. The ratings were persistently poor and if they didn't improve, it would not be long before Radio Haxford dropped the programme.

As we came though Easter and looked forward to the beginning of May and the much anticipated coronation of His Majesty, beyond which we could savour the coming of summer, I told myself I wasn't worried. I had a cast iron contract which still had a year and a half to run.

In truth, the financial aspect of my Radio Haxford deal was no longer critical. We faced the same issues as other people: the cost of living crisis, the ever-spiralling price of energy, and so on, but we were fairly well-cushioned against them because Dennis was back at work six days a week and our income was where it had been before The Incident.

For all you newbies, The Incident was our name for the evening, a year in the past, when two men working for a political hopeful, beat my husband up so badly that they broke both his legs, fractured his skull, and left him dependent on others (me most of the time) for months on end. He was fully recovered aside from tricky knees which meant he relied on a stick if he had to walk too far, and occasional glitches in his speech, which could be an indicator of his stress levels, but which were deliberate most of the time, designed to enhance his auto-obsessed eccentricity.

So if not the money I made from Radio Haxford what did concern me about the potential removal of me from the airwaves?

It was a difficult question to answer.

Well, it wasn't, but I didn't want to accept the answer which stared me in the face, and it took a new case to force that conclusion upon me.

It was all prompted by an email which arrived out of the blue. I was suspicious, naturally, and I didn't know it then, but it would lead me into one of the most intriguing, and in many ways, disturbing episodes I'd ever come across.

Let me take you back to those final, showery days of April.

Chapter One

Regardless of the questionable ratings, we were still recording Christine Capper's Mystery Hour every week, and one of my biggest problems was digging out the mysteries for me to talk about.

To begin with, the ratings dip left me with little enthusiasm for the task and to make matters worse, the ideas came from my old cases, most of which were not mysteries. For example, there was no great puzzle behind the regular, Thursday meetings between Mr I'm High On A Viagra Overdose and Ms Give Me Everything You've Got And I'll Still Come Back For More, but that was hardly the kind of story which would appeal to the diehard, old-fashioned Radio Haxford audience… at least not according to the powers that be it wasn't. And even if it was, I couldn't go into great detail because I *never* went into detail. Sometimes I took a statement from them for the injured party's solicitor, but most of the time, I simply photographed them arriving at the Sleaze Pit Hotel at the same time every Thursday afternoon, and presented the evidence – along with the bill for my time and effort – to the husband/wife/partner/significant other on the wrong end of the infidelity.

Similarly when Snuggles the dog went missing,

my first port of call, and quite often the last because that's usually where I found him/her/it, was to the Haxford Animal Rescue Centre off Huddersfield Road.

Eric Reitman, our producer and director didn't worry about such trivia as a case lacking in mystery. He told me to dress the stories up a little. In other words, exaggerate, tell a few lies. That went against my principles and the underlying premise upon which the show was supposed to be built: i.e. the truth.

There was another aspect of the job I found niggling. After dredging up the cases, I had to draft an account which would then be presented to our scriptwriter, Jill Bleaker. Preparing the precis usually meant a full day's work for me, and considering the audience reaction to the show, it peeved.

Throughout a chilly March and damp April (we could hardly expect subtropical temperatures at that time of year, could we?) while Dennis kept one eye on the energy bills, Eric kept telling me that the Mystery Hour's rating was consistent by which he meant the gradient was consistent: downhill, and both he and I believed it was only a matter of time before the station pulled the plug. Even with Dennis back at work, I wasn't sure where that would leave us. I'm not saying we were in desperate need of the money, but it came in useful, especially with bills that were only just shy of your common or garden monthly mortgage repayment.

On a nippy Wednesday coming up to the end of April, Eric was at pains to reassure me. "You have a contract, Chrissy, and you haven't breached it. If Radio Haxford decide to drop the show, they're breaking the agreement and they have to pay you or give you another show to present. Personally, I'd still rather see the format change."

Throughout the months of threat, he had insisted it was the mysteries and not me personally which the listeners did not like. They were old hat, familiar to my blog/vlog audience.

"The Great British public has an affinity with mysteries which borders on obsession," he once told me, "but they don't like this one, and being Yorkshire, they're not slow to say why. We need to do something different, something that will capture the listeners' imagination, but don't ask me what that might be. I have no ideas."

It was about that time when I got involved in the Allbrook/Keogh business, and at the same time, Dennis and I travelled to Cambridge for my niece's wedding and we became embroiled in the murder there, and it gave me the idea of investigative campaigning. Negative outcomes of both cases put me off the idea before it ever reached the ears of the big boss and it never went any further.

Dennis, on the other hand, was full of ideas. "You need summat to make your punters think, lass," he said when I told him of Eric's opinion. "I had this Renault, a bit like your old motor, and every so often the wipers, flashers, heater would just stop working. The lad who owned it had to turn the engine off and back on again to get 'em going. Electrical fault and me and Grimy tried everything but we couldn't crack it. Anyway, we did it in the end. Know what it was?"

"A little man under the bonnet ordering all the electrical bobbins to down tools?"

You would think my sarcastic tone would have got through to Dennis, but he just frowned at me. "That's daft."

"No dafter than you suggesting mysterious engine complaints for my listeners. People want to hear about crime, Dennis, not tricky Renault engines."

"There were nowt wrong with the engine. It was the—"

"You know what I mean."

And with that caustic comment, he shut up.

It was all very much on my mind on the morning of Tuesday, April 25th when I sat in the conservatory, a small fan heater keeping my feet warm, while I worked on an account of the McCruddens' case, the one which got Dennis beaten up. I had to cut it to the bone. To tell the whole story would require four or five hours, and I was restricted to forty-two minutes. It meant cutting to the chase and eliminating so many of my Conan Doyle-esque deductions.

And the fan heater? According to Dennis, even with the weather warming up a little, we still couldn't afford to turn on the central heating until after eleven in the morning when we switched to off-peak rates. I think it was just my husband's native, Yorkshire tight-fistedness showing through, but I have to say that the numbers on the smart meter went round so fast they reminded me of a petrol pump when I was filling up the car.

The task at hand was not going well. I was due at the Radio Haxford studio by half past ten for my weekly agony aunt spot, and Cappy the Cat was eating into my time, constantly demanding to be let out. Not that he actually set foot out of the door. I would abandon the laptop, open the door for him and he would take a sniff at the rain, then glower up at me for making the weather so bad, before stomping off to his dish, and on finding that empty he would disappear in the direction of the front room and his bed. When it came to eating and sulking it was a toss-up who was worse: Dennis or Cappy the Cat.

With the time coming up to nine o'clock, I abandoned the precis, saved the work so far, and headed for the kettle. A brace of chocolate digestives to go with my cup of tea might not do my fluctuating weight any favours but I felt sure they would enhance my creativity.

While I waited for the kettle to boil, I heard the familiar beep of an incoming email. Spam, I diagnosed without even seeing it. I wasn't expecting anything, and like most people I tended to get more nuisance mail than genuine. I had a business email. Of course I did. And it was in the public domain. It had to be. No point advertising your services as a private investigator if you don't put up contact details. I also had a couple of webmail addresses and they took most of the spam, but it had to be said that one or two did occasionally make it to my main address.

And it was to that address that I went first and sure enough, it was spam. 'FAO Christine Capper', it read, and there was a video file attached to it.

I was on the point of deleting it, when a twin beep from my smartphone announced a text message. Dennis, I would bet. And he would be asking what was for tea that evening. I think it helped him decide what to have for breakfast at Haxford Mill. No, it didn't. He always had a full English for breakfast at Haxford Mill.

I was wrong anyway. The text had nothing to do with Dennis. It was from an unknown number, or should I say a number unknown to my phone, and it read, '*I've just sent you an email which you will no doubt dump as spam but it's not. It's about a miscarriage of justice. Please check it out. Scan the video for malware, by all means, but do watch it.*' It was signed, *A Friend.*

Yes. Thank you. I'll pass. Marking him down as persistent son of the sod, I deleted the text and followed up by deleting the email, too.

Ten minutes later, working on the by-election case again, struggling to decide whether or not I should include reference to my interview with the odds-on favourite candidate (he did win by a landslide) the phone began chirping for attention.

The number was (again) unknown, but as a private eye I was used to that. All my clients tended to that level of discretion. I made the connection and announced myself. "Christine Capper."

"Did you watch the video?"

I'd come across some persistent spammers in my time, but this guy was Olympic standard. "Who are you?" I demanded.

"I can't tell you that, and if you watch the video

8

and you're half the private eye your website claims you to be, you should be able to work out why I can't tell you. Just watch it."

And with that he cut the call off.

I seethed at his audacity for a moment and I was tempted to call him back, but thought better of it. I had more on my plate than dealing with people like him. Instead, various epithets ran through my mind, most of them suitable for a 21st century celebrity like me, but not for a 20th century lady like me.

Then my thinking ground to a halt. Yes, I had known some persistent men in my time, but not on this scale. Fellow private eye, Nathan Kalinsky, for example, was persistent in his flattery, the build-up to an attempt at getting me laid beneath him in the moorland grasses (he failed). Dennis was persistent in his efforts to make me his wife (he succeeded). Ingrid canvassed my support for her career as a singer (she failed) and Simon persisted in hounding me for my blessing when he joined the police after university (he succeeded). None of them had insisted I watch a video first, and although Nathan was a stranger to me when he first showed up, I soon got to know him. Dennis and I were living together before we married so I knew who he was, and I for obvious reasons I knew my son and daughter.

With this in mind, armed with tea and chocolate digestives, I recovered the email. The return address was total nonsense. N.O.Bodee and a webmail address. The message had no text other than, '*please watch*' and the attached video. I ran a virus and malware scan, which came back clean and finally opened the attachment.

I recognised the scenario right away. Two detectives interviewing a suspect, and it occurred to me why he couldn't tell me who or what he was. It could have been a set-up, a theatrical group at work, but in the light of Mr X's persistence, I didn't think so. In my opinion, this was an official police recording of an interview, and for it to come to me was strictly against every rule in the police book. He shouldn't have sent it and I shouldn't be watching it. The sender had to be a police officer, and by the very act of passing this to me, he was risking his career.

I also suspected that if I carried on watching, it might put me at risk of prosecution. By rights, I should have taken it to the police station and handed it over.

As I sat there, munching on McVities finest, I paused the video while I thought about the rights and wrongs of the situation, part of his text message echoed though my fluttering brain. *It's about a miscarriage of justice.*

How could I not watch it?

I hovered the cursor over the 'play' icon and hesitated. Thirty years ago, I was a beat bobby, a community constable, and ignoring that, I had always been an upright, law-abiding citizen. When Ingrid was about thirteen, I caught her with a pack of expensive makeup. She didn't have the money for such a purchase, I hadn't bought it, so I knew she had stolen it from Boots or Superdrug or somewhere like that. When I pressured her, she admitted it.

I never believed in corporal punishment, but I gave her a smack anyway, and grounded her for a month. I manhandled her into the car, drove her into town, and compelled her to hand it over and apologise for stealing it. The store manager appreciated my actions, and he was very sorry, but company policy left him with no option. Ingrid was reported for shoplifting. I used a little influence at the police station, and she got away with a caution on the grounds that she had handed the goods back and shown due contrition.

That sense of right and wrong had been with me all my life. Good heavens, I wouldn't even steal odd toffees from the pick 'n' mix display in CutCost. And now, here I sat debating whether to watch an illegal download or do the right thing and take it to the police.

It was those few words, *a miscarriage of justice,* which tormented me. I believed in right not wrong, so was it right to do wrong in order to put right something that was wrong?

There were so many 'rights' and 'wrongs' in that last paragraph that I had to take five minutes and another chocolate digestive to stop my head from spinning. That's my excuse anyway.

I reached a decision. If I watched it and dismissed it as nonsense, I could take it the police later and plead ignorance and/or idiocy as my excuse for watching it. My good friend Detective Sergeant Amanda Hiscoe would understand.

And with that, I clicked the 'play' button.

The date and time stamp indicated early March

and half past two in the afternoon. The two police officers identified themselves first. DCI Harold Nocton and Detective Sergeant Bentil, whose first name I didn't catch, but sounded like Karachi. I would later learn that it was Kaatachi and he was of Ghanaian descent. Nocton, I guessed, would have suffered when he was a younger, junior officer. Nicknames are endemic in Haxford. Some people still referred to me as Capper the Copper, and Dennis was (inevitably) Cappy. I could see that Nocton would have been known as Knock On. I guessed him to be in his fifties, and Bentil twenty or so years younger and although the interview took place in a recognisable police station interview room, both men declared themselves to be from Scotland Yard.

The suspect identified himself as Derek Tyndall. Subsequent research would show that he was in his late forties, but he looked a good deal older; a factor of his bushy, greying beard and crinkly mop of hair, augmented by the crow's feet around his red-rimmed eyes. A career burglar to judge from the early discussion, he looked to be short of stature, thin and wiry, and in my opinion, perfectly built for housebreaking. I could imagine those veined hands and nimble fingers working expertly at locks new and not so new, and I could visualise the narrow arms pulling on a crowbar while sweat broke out on the wrinkled brow.

I noted that Tyndall did not have a lawyer present, and it soon became clear why as Nocton led the session.

"Mr Tyndall, you were apprehended breaking

into factory premises off Archway Road and you've been charged and remanded for that offence. Sergeant Bentil and I are concerned with certain comments you made during the interview at which you were charged. You asked for a number of other offences to be taken into consideration amongst which was a break in at Fairburn House, over Easter weekend, twenty years ago. A job which you claim you carried out with the assistance of Jack Prater."

"That's right."

"According to official records, on the night in question, Prater was in Haxford, West Yorkshire, murdering a young woman named Rebecca Walmer. He's serving life for killing her."

Tyndall helped himself to a slug of tea. "He was shafted."

"So you claim. How come he didn't own up to Fairburn House in his defence?"

The prisoner laughed. "What? And sell me down the swanee? It ain't just you lot who club together, you know. So do we. No one was fingered for the Fairburn job, and if he'd opened his mouth in court, he would have dropped me in it. We don't do that kinda stuff."

"He confessed to the Walmer killing," Sergeant Bentil pointed out.

Tyndall found this equally funny. "How long have you been with the filth? You're a big bugger too. Don't tell me you ain't roughed a few guys up to get them to cough to a job they haven't done. I meanersay, just cos I TIC'd all those jobs, don't mean to say I did 'em."

TIC was familiar to me. It was short for 'taken

13

into consideration' a means by which anyone charged with an offence could clear out a backlog of other crimes, and he could never be prosecuted for them in the future.

Tyndall was still talking. "Your boys showed me a list of blags they wanted clearing off their books. I'm going down for a stretch, no two ways about it, and they've already promised that if I own up to 'em, they'll go easy. They reckon I'll get two years. Easy money and I'll be out in a year."

I knew there was time when such a practice was common. It was means of clearing the backlog of unsolved crimes, but by the time I joined the police it had largely been stamped out. A good thing, too I'd never been a fan of lazy policing.

Unfazed by the revelation, Nocton was nevertheless unwilling to let it go so easily. "And how do we know that you're not taking the Fairburn House job into consideration as a favour to the police?"

For the first time, Tyndall appeared irritated. He pointed a nicotine-stained finger at the table top. "We did it, pal. Me and Jack Prater. We turned that place over."

"All right. Tell me about the gear you got away with." The inspector tossed his pen on the table and sat back waiting for an answer.

"Silverware, bitta jewellery, some cash out the safe." Tyndall laughed again. "Safe? He'd have been better off with a piggy bank. That lock was so easy it was—"

"How much cash?"

The interruption did not faze the prisoner.

"Over a grand, close on twelve hundred nicker as I remember. Me and Jack, we split that 50-50 there and then. Five hundred and summink dabs apiece, and I would have sent him the rest of his share when I collected a couple of weeks later, after I fenced the rest of the gear, but a day or two after we did Fairburns, the filth up north had him for killing this tart."

Nocton continued to press. "So there was cash. What about the other stuff you stole? Anything remarkable?"

Tyndall's malleable features screwed up into a passable impression of someone struggling to recall. He crushed out his cigarette. "Bitta tom...tom foolery—" (old slang for jewellery) "—know what I mean? There was a few bitsa china. Quality stuff, mind, not your market stall crap, and the thing that really stands out was this photograph frame. Silver, it was. Had all these fancy patterns round it. I got rid of the picture, natch. It was of some geezer, probably the old boy what owned the place, and he was with a flashy bint. Maybe his missus. I don't know, do I? Come on, pal, you're asking me about a blag from nearly twenty years ago."

"Okay. Final question. How can you be so sure of the date?"

"Two things. Like you said, it was Easter weekend. They was away, the people what owned the place. We knew in advance they would be. And second, like I told you, your boys up north nicked Jacko the following day, and I was on pins when they got him, because I was expecting him to cough to the Fairburn job as his alibi. But he's a good lad,

15

is Jack. He wouldn't grass me up, and there was no way I'd come forward to get him out of the cow crap, because if the boot was on the other foot, he'd carry on just the same as I did. Only real mates would do that for you." Tyndall jabbed his finger into the table top. "I'm telling you, pal, Jacko was railroaded for snuffing that girl."

Chapter Two

From the moment they mentioned her name, the case of Rebecca Walmer's murder flooded into my mind. It was, as DCI Nocton said, about twenty years back, and it sent a shockwave of horror and anger throughout Haxford. We had our share or killings, naturally, but even taking into account later cases, some of which I was involved with, no one could remember one so callous and pointless as Becky's.

To ensure I recalled everything properly, I looked the case up in the archives of the Haxford Recorder's website, and I was right.

Becky was just nineteen years of age, her whole life ahead of her, a pretty young woman who had the kind of figure I'd sell Dennis to possess, and whose smile radiated that *joie de vivre* common to teenagers. Her parents, along with her younger brother, were enjoying the Easter weekend away in Mablethorpe. On Saturday night, Becky was out with friends, partying, clubbing. She got home about half past one in the morning and disturbed a burglar who had already beaten the family dog to death. He strangled her and fled.

Easter was late that year, towards the end of April, and a neighbour – who to this day had never been named – out walking his dog at half past six the following morning, noticed the door was open. He knew the family were away so he went in to ensure everything was all right, only to find Becky's body laid prone alongside the mangled dog on the front room carpet.

Senior Investigating Officer was DI Peter Kitson from Huddersfield, and within twenty-four hours, he arrested Jack Prater, who like Tyndall, was a career burglar, and well-known throughout the Haxford area. He was also a man with a history of low-key violence: i.e. thumping the odd householder who disturbed him while he was ransacking their homes. He had never been known to commit murder, but after less than forty-eight hours of interrogation, he confessed, was charged and remanded. That was on Easter Monday. Six months later, he faced judge and jury, and retracted his confession. He maintained that it was made under duress, but he couldn't back up his claim. Kitson and his sidekick, Detective Sergeant Frank Penning, were adamant that they had followed the rules, and the taped interviews backed up their side of the story. Prater was jailed for life, and according to the Recorder, he was still locked away in Wakefield prison, still refusing to acknowledge his guilt, and showing no signs of remorse.

I remembered that Prater's family suffered a lot of abuse after his arrest and again after his conviction. It was mostly verbal, some of it physical, as in assaults on his partner (whose name I couldn't remember and which was kept out of the press for her safety) and his two children. '*They must have known'*, was the general feeling in Haxford, and although I disapproved of the abuse heaped upon the family, I agreed with the sentiments. Becky was strangled with a fine ligature, so there was no blood loss from her, but the family pet, a golden retriever named Tigger, was beaten to death and Prater must have been spattered with the dog's blood when he got home that night. Don't tell me his partner didn't question it, don't tell me she didn't twig when she read the reports of Becky's murder.

All in all, then, it appeared to be a shocking but routine open and shut case, and that was the form with murder inquiries. Most were solved in a matter of days. Those that were not, tended to go on for weeks, months, even years.

The email, text, and brief, irascible phone call I'd received said different, and so did Derek Tyndall. I had no doubt that Jack Prater would, too. So was it possible that Kitson and Penning conspired to frame Prater?

I didn't know Kitson well for two reasons.

First, Haxford is a small town, and did not warrant the permanent presence of an inspector. On such occasions as one was needed it fell upon Huddersfield to supply him or her. It was the very reason why DI Paddy Quinn, a Haxforder by birth, moved to Huddersfield when he was promoted, much to the relief of everyone at Haxford Police Station, I might add.

Second, I'd left the police at the time of Becky's murder. Yes, I had met and had dealings with Kitson when I was still on the force, but never for very long. He was CID, I was uniformed, and us uniforms had little to do with the top drawer detectives, except when they told us to get down on our knees for a fingertip search, or had us chasing round the station bringing them files, messages, statements, cups of tea, chocolate Hob Nobs (the very thought sent me to the McVities pack again) and all the other, essential elements necessary to keep our wannabe Sherlocks in peak condition.

Again the question ran round my head. Was it possible that the two officers had framed Jack Prater?

That was a question I could not answer. My impression of Kitson was of a loudmouth, but an honest loudmouth. Yes he would apply pressure, yes he would never back down from asking awkward questions, demanding answers whether or not the suspect was inclined to speak, whether or not the suspect's brief insisted on his client's silence, but as far as my limited knowledge of him stretched, Kitson did so within the rules.

His bagman, Detective Sergeant Penning was an unknown to me. Well, I say unknown. I knew of him, but I couldn't recall ever having dealings with him. It's like when I was a child and mother would tell me about Great Uncle Arnold, a man who survived the carnage of the Somme, a man who was considered a family hero. I never met Great Uncle Arnold. I wouldn't recognise him if I ran over him on Sheffield Road, but I knew of him, and the same could be said of Frank Penning. Like Kitson, he was based in Huddersfield and the inspector brought him along for the Walmer case. It was the one area where Paddy Quinn and Kitson differed. Kitson trained Paddy, and our current inspector considered Kitson his hero and role model, but when Paddy came to Haxford he always conscripted Mandy Hiscoe as his sidekick.

When her name chimed in my head, my thoughts automatically turned to Mandy.

Notwithstanding our age difference (she was thirty-six/seven to my fifty-four) we were good friends, and yet we never served together. She signed on a good number of years after I left the police, but I got to know her through my other contacts at the station, and from the off, we were the best of besties.

A single mother by choice, she was an able detective, and by rights, she should have been promoted to inspector, but that would involve a move to Huddersfield or Dewsbury, and she preferred working in Haxford, so she consistently refused to take the inspector's course and exam. She was quite content to carry on as a sergeant.

As well as being local, well briefed on the happenings, criminal or otherwise in Haxford, she had the advantage in that she worked with Kitson when she was a DC. If anyone knew anything about the potential for Kitson and Penning having framed Jack Prater, it would be Mandy, and yet, I was hesitant to ring her. She would want to know where I came by the information.

Frustration flooded through me and threatened to burst out. As matters stood, she was the only person I could speak to about the Walmer case and she was also the worst person I could speak to.

Even so, I had to know. If there was any validity to Derek Tyndall's assertion, then the Met would have already passed the information to West Yorkshire and (theoretically) they would be investigating. In which case, why did Mr X send the video to me, why the text, why the call insisting that I watch it? There was only one explanation and it did not bring me any comfort: West Yorkshire knew all right, and they were sitting on it, ignoring it in the hope that it would just go away, and Mr X knew that because, as I had deduced earlier, he was a police officer. The moment I opened up to Mandy, she would want the bottom line and if I refused, she could legitimately accuse me of withholding information.

I had no choice I decided as I made myself a fresh cup of tea and opened the door once more for Cappy the Cat. It would have to be Mandy or like the top dogs at West Yorkshire police, ignore it altogether, and my inbuilt sense of justice, not to mention my innate tendency for poking my nose in, would not let me drop it. Our moody moggie still didn't fancy the rain and came back as I settled down in the kitchen this time, with my tea and smartphone.

"Haxford police, Sergeant Hiscoe speaking."

I tried to keep my voice bright and cheerful. "Morning, Mandy. It's Chrissy."

"Whatever you want, the answer is no."

We can all be moody in the spring, eager for the start of the coming summer, but I did wonder if some date had let her down. On the other hand, it was more likely that... "Darlene playing you up, is she?" Darlene was her nine-month-old daughter.

"What do you want, Chrissy?"

"Well, it's coming to something when I can't ring an old friend and suggest meeting for tea and teacakes after my radio slot."

Her mood changed instantly. "You are a lifesaver. Twelve o'clock at Terry's?"

"Be there or be forever crossed off my Christmas card list."

I ended the call with a gleeful chuckle, checked the clock, read a few minutes to ten. Shock, horror! I was due at the Radio Haxford studio by half past. I had less than fifteen minutes before I needed to leave. My eleven o'clock slot comprised fifteen minutes in the middle of Reggie Monk's morning show, but I was supposed to be there half an hour early so the team could brief me on potential controversial issues. If I didn't get a move on I would be late.

I dashed through to the bedroom so fast that Cappy the Cat must have thought the house was on fire and came haring after me. When he found me throwing off my scruffs and sliding into a pair of denims and a woolly jumper, he gave me a glower which read, 'typical, just ruddy typical', and slinked off back to the front room.

Less than a quarter of an hour later, I climbed into my car and drove off down to Haxford.

The two lost friends programmes and the ailing Christine Capper's Mystery Hour were recorded every Wednesday in my conservatory on the grounds that there wasn't really room at the studio which was located on the upper gallery of Haxford

23

Market Hall. The agony aunt spot, however, went out live and I had to share the tiny studio with Reggie Monk and his halitosis and general body odour. Not a pleasant prospect but I was only in there for fifteen minutes and the pay was good. After the spot, there was a compulsory fifteen-minute debrief during which Eric Reitman would give me the bouquets and brickbats. Mercifully and unlike the mystery hour, there had always been more of the former than the latter.

The queries were always the same, too. Relationships, addictions, debt, and I didn't have to find the answers. The crew did that prior to my going live, and all I had to do was read the answers from a tablet in front of me and dress them up in my own inimitable style. Lately there had been an increasing number of questions on coping with bad weather and ever rising energy bills. 'Turn the flaming heating off and put another two jumpers on' would be Dennis's solution, but along with suggesting they try to stick to off-peak hours, I referred listeners to the power companies' advice pages, and if they were having problems meeting the bills, speak to their supplier. *Only don't call them a set of thieving so-and-so's.* That last thought often sneaked into my mind as I was giving out that last bit of advice.

As it happened, Terry's Tea Bar, where I was due to meet Mandy, was also located in the market hall, but on the ground floor, and I made no apologies for being one of his most loyal customers. Terry did the most succulent toasted teacakes in West Yorkshire, possibly the country... even

Europe. And every cup of tea was like a well-kept Mouton-Rothschild... the wines, I mean. I don't think Chateau Mouton-Rothschild produced teabags.

I had many a meeting at Terry's, some of them with Eric, including one where he persuaded me to sign up for the mystery hour. I anticipated another get together any day soon, one where he would tear up the contract, but for now, it was Mandy Hiscoe's turn.

I left the studio at half past eleven and with thirty minutes to kill, I had a wander round various stalls where I picked up a few essential groceries, and other vital necessities; eye shadow, underwear for the coming summer, and a new sweater in red, with a delightful, floral motif across the front.

I got to Terry's bang on twelve o'clock to find Mandy settling in at a table with her tea and teacake. It was no surprise. I had to drive a mile and bit to get to Haxford. All she had to do was walk the five hundred yards from the police station. On the other hand, I was only in the studio fifty yards away. All right then, so she wasn't a shopaholic and I was.

She greeted me with a tired smile. "How's life as a radio superstar?"

"Busy every Tuesday and Wednesday, but otherwise, easy. How about life with plod?"

"It never changes."

I went to the counter, ordered and collected my toasted teacake and tea and joined her.

One look at her mean face told me that no matter how much I pussyfooted around, she would lose it when I got to the nitty gritty, so I fired the opening shots right away. "What can you tell me about the murder of Becky Walmer—"

That was as far as I got before she cut me off. "Hang on. I thought this was two old pals enjoying tea and cakes."

I indicated the plates. "We are enjoying tea and teacakes. Come on, Mandy, I'm in radio now. I might not be a big wheel influencer like they get on social media, but I do have listeners and I'm gaining traction." A pause to savour a bite of teacake. "I've heard whispers."

It didn't seem possible, but her face darkened further. "What whispers?"

"Don't tell me you don't know—"

All of a sudden she stopped being my friend and became the professional police officer. "I do know, but I want to know what you've heard and where you heard it from."

I laughed the objection off. "We stars of radio never reveal our sources."

"Chrissy..." There was a warning edge to her voice.

"Come off it, Mandy, it's just a whisper. That's all."

She jabbed an angry finger into the table top. "If your Simon's telling tales out of school—"

It was my turn to interrupt and in tones as brittle as hers. Simon was my son and a detective constable, and I resented her accusation. "It didn't come from Simon. He's even tighter with information than you and Paddy. My information didn't come from anyone linked to the Haxford police... Well, I don't think it did. But if it's anything like true, Jack Prater has been inside for twenty years for a crime he didn't commit."

"Bullplop." Silence reigned for a moment, but when she spoke again, Mandy was cooler. "We heard about it three weeks ago—"

It was my turn to cut her off. "And yet you kept it quiet."

"We had to. All right?" She leaned forward to make sure I got the message. "Paddy gave it a couple of coats of looking at, and then got a call to see the Chief Superintendent who told him in no uncertain terms that it was twaddle. We were ordered to ignore it until such times as fresh evidence, reliable evidence, comes forward. The hoo-hah stemmed from an interview in London with a scroat named Del Tyndall."

I almost cut in and told her I knew, but common sense took over and I kept my mouth shut. Unusual, yes, but I managed it.

"Tyndall is a pro burglar and has more form than a three-times Grand National winner," she went on. "His word doesn't constitute evidence. You used to be one of us, so you know the score. Tyndall and Jacko Prater have been buddies since forever. They were walled up together in Winson Green, Birmingham, about a year before Becky was murdered. As far as we're concerned, this whisper you've heard is more likely Tyndall trying to get his old pal off the hook and ruin Pete Kitson's reputation. We can't take Tyndall's word for it. We need evidence and we don't have any."

She was running out of breath and irritation so she paused to take in a healthy swallow of tea and a couple of deep breaths. I realised that it wasn't just me winding her up, and I couldn't lay the blame at her police work. The levels of stress, the pressure under which they worked was consistent, and Mandy had always coped. It had to be...

"Is Darlene teething or something?"

She nodded. "She's driving me up the wall with it. They do, don't they?"

"You have to look at it from her angle, Mandy. It's like having a permanent ache in your jaw. Is she okay otherwise?"

"Yes. Fine. She's a darling, Darlene." For the first time since I arrived, she smiled. "I don't know what I'd do without her, but I'd be glad to see the back of the crying and dribbling, and she bites and sucks on anything. Even when I put teething gel on her gums, she bites down on my fingers."

I smiled, too. "Been there, done that, bought the T-shirt. Twice." I reached across the table and took her hand. "It goes with the territory, luv, but you just said something which makes it all worth it. You don't know what you'd do without her?" I sat back and sipped tea. "Anyway, I thought your mam looks after her while you're working."

"She does and she's more used to it than me. Don't forget, I have two brothers and a sister, so Ma's been there four times."

"If it's any consolation, you'll have forgotten this conversation in fifteen years. By then, she'll be a gadabout teenager determined to go her own way and you'll be fighting her every inch of the way."

This time it was a grunty little laugh. "I'm already looking forward to it." She, too, took some tea. "Now, come on, Chrissy. Stop trying to blindside me. What's this about Jack Prater?"

"I told you. It was a whisper. That's all."

Suspicion clouded her features. "Has Elaine Anguage hired you?"

Puzzlement clouded mine. "Who's Elaine Anguage?"

"Prater's partner back then."

The penny dropped right away. I never could remember her name. Odd when it was such a curious surname, too.

Mandy was still talking. "She had a couple of kids by him. Last I heard, she was living on Batley Road Estate. She's been screaming for years that Jacko didn't do it."

"Has she now? Well, to answer your question, no she has not hired me. I don't even know the woman. And to be completely honest, when I heard the tale, I said exactly what you've just said to me. It's nonsense. I mean I didn't know Kitson well, and he always came across as a bit gobby, but I considered him honest."

I cast a furtive glance around to make sure no one was listening. A pointless exercise. There was one other customer in the café and she was three tables away. Behind the counter, Terry and his two assistants were idling away the time, chatting.

Nevertheless, I lowered my voice. "Do you know, when I was on the force, he tried to get me into bed. Said if I was good to him, he'd help me get a leg up."

"Snap," Mandy said. "A leg up for a legover. How did you react?"

"I told him exactly where he could go. You know me, Mandy. I don't use bad language, but I made an exception that one time."

"Snap," she repeated. "I told him exactly where he could stick it. I even offered to show him where and I'd switch the electricity on once he was firmly stuck in the wall socket." We both tittered like schoolgirls. "Thing is, Chrissy, he never held it against me. He tried it with most of the women at one time or another, but when they told him no thanks, which most of them did, he didn't take the hump. He never held any woman back because she refused him."

"Not an issue with me," I said. "As you know, I wasn't interested in CID and he had no say over uniformed. He's retired now, isn't he?"

She nodded. "Must be three or four years back since he went. He bought a place on the Costa del Copper. Somewhere near Estepona. Him and his missus." She snapped back to the present. "He was straight as a dye, Pete Kitson. He nailed Prater for Becky's murder, but he did it honestly."

"According to the Recorder, Prater confessed."

"He did, and he retracted his confession during his trial. Jury didn't believe him and he got life while Kitson got a slap on the back from the top brass." She drank her tea and glanced at her watch. "Five minutes and I have to go, so come clean, Chrissy. Where did you hear and what's going down?"

"I'm not going to name my informant, but he said you people are sitting on it."

"Well now you know. And I suppose you're

going to poke your nose in?"

I gave her an ingratiating smile. "As if I would. Seriously, Mandy, now that I know who she is, I'll be speaking to Prater's partner, this Elaine Anguage, see what she has to say, and I'll take it from there."

"Is this to do with Reitman at Radio Haxford? Word is the mystery hour isn't doing well."

Mandy was as good as me at jumping to the wrong conclusion, so I stayed silent. Better to let her think it was down to Eric Reitman rather than me watching official, albeit pirated videos.

She wasn't done. "Listen, I can't stop you, but you should tell Eric to watch his step. If you get anything, anything at all, you bring it to me because if Paddy catches on, he'll throw the book at you, Reitman, Radio Haxford and anyone else he can think of who happens to be in range."

"Because Kitson was Paddy's hero."

"Precisely."

Chapter Three

The niggly interlude with Mandy served a few useful purposes. First, it confirmed that the local police were aware of Tyndall's allegation. Second, it confirmed the sender's accusation that the West Yorkshire force was sitting on it for lack of fresh evidence, which underscored my assumption that my mysterious contact was a police officer. Third, and most important from my point of view, it gave me the name of Jack Prater's partner. Elaine Anguage. All I had to do was find out where on Batley Road Estate she lived.

Fortunately, I had another good friend, Kim Aspinall who, along with her older partner, Alden Upley, ran the public library, and she had ways of digging out such information, not all of them within the constraints or the spirit of the Data Protection Act.

The library was situated on the four-way junction of Yorkshire Street, High Street and Batley Way, which conveniently led to Batley Road where Batley Road Estate was located, and after half an hour with Kim, who kept looking over her shoulder to ensure Alden was not watching, she found Elaine Anguage's address for me.

Both Batley Way and Batley Road were

strangely named. Neither of them led to Batley, which is a small town between Dewsbury and Morley, to the north and east of Huddersfield. In other words, nowhere near Haxford. Even worse was the naming of the streets on Batley Road Estate. All but one was named after famous battles involving the British: Agincourt, Sebastopol, Waterloo, Mafeking. The odd one out was Versailles Crescent. According to my research Versailles was where the treaty which marked the official end of WW1 was signed, and the only reference I ever found to the Battle of Versailles was a fashion show in 1973. Since Batley Road Estate was built in the late sixties, it seemed unlikely to commemorate fighting on the catwalk, and no one at the town hall could explain the discrepancy.

It was at number 61 Versailles Crescent that I found Elaine Anguage and her two children, Teddy and Wynn. I say children, but both were around thirtyish. Since Elaine was barely fifty and her incarcerated husband was only forty-eight, I guessed they must have started young. Both offspring still lived at home, which I found odd. Perish the thought of Simon and Ingrid still living with us. I had enough trouble with them when they were in their teens. Even more curious were the Anguage offspring's names. Contrary to my automatic assumption, Teddy was christened Teddy and not Edward, while Wynn was Wynn, and not short for Wynette or Winifred.

All three had the same problem, however. They were thin to the point of emaciation, and I felt a pang of envy as I followed Teddy into the three-bedroom flat. If I had that kind of metabolism, I wouldn't need to worry about the number of chocolate digestives I put away.

Weight was not the only thing they had in common. Each of them burned with anger at the very mention of the (perceived) injustice done to Jack.

"He was innocent," Elaine declared after I gave her a vague explanation for my unexpected visit. "I told 'em then, I've been telling 'em ever since, and they don't take no notice. And now you're saying you've got proof of that?"

A small, bony woman, barely five feet tall, with a straggle of dark hair around her underfed features, she reminded me of my grandmother on my father's side. Old Lily was just as fierce, frightened of no one, but she was also very deaf which led to any number of arguments when she misheard something, most of the time when she was talking with granddad. He was a huge strapping man, again scared of nothing and no one, but he would suffer the wrath of God if he didn't take his working boots off before he walked into the house.

Teddy and Wynn were suspicious of me. I could see it in their faces, especially when Wynn's lips curled as she delivered tea in a beaker that looked as if it hadn't seen a drop of Fairy Liquid since... oh I don't know... since the Treaty of Versailles was signed?

Suppressing a grimace at the tea, which I felt contained enough tannin to unblock the drains of every bungalow on Bracken Close, I hastened to correct Elaine. "I don't have proof, luv. I've heard a whisper. That's all. I know it's a long time ago, but are you able to account for Jack's whereabouts on the night Becky Walmer was murdered?"

"Course I can, I mean course I can. He was on a job down south somewhere. Got home about five in the morning. She was throttled no later than half past one, so the filth reckoned. It wasn't him."

"And did you tell the police that?"

Teddy answered for his mother. "She did. I remember it. She said it in court, too."

"They reckoned I was lying to cover for him, but I was telling 'em the truth for once. It wasn't my Jacko what did that girl."

I concentrated on Teddy. "You must have been very young."

"I was about ten years old. All right, so I was still a kid, but I remember Dad getting home. It was Easter and we were supposed to be going to the seaside for the day. Then the filth carted him off to the nick and the next thing we knew, he was walled up for life."

Although it sounded like the truth, Teddy's words didn't make a lot of sense. If Jack had driven through the night to get home from somewhere north of London, he would hardly have enough energy to take them to Scarborough or Blackpool unless he planned to sleep it off in a deckchair while they rode the beach donkeys and threw their pocket money away on the machines in the arcades.

I focussed on Elaine. "The problem is, Mrs Prater—"

"It's Miss, and it's not Prater, it's Anguage."

"I'm sorry, Ms Anguage. The problem is, you have no definitive proof of Jack's whereabouts during the night. He might tell you he was down south, but you can't confirm that."

"No, but I can tell you he handed over the better part of five hundred sovs, and he didn't get that from the Walmers' place. They're like us. They've been skint all their lives."

"But you didn't tell the police that?"

"Knowing where Jacko got it from, would you?"

"You don't know about that little tramp, either, do you?" Wynn said. The suspicion and resentment were still there, dripping from every word, like rain pouring through a roof with a dozen slates missing.

"Tramp? You mean Becky?"

"She was anyone's for a half of lager and a vodka kick."

"You obviously knew her," I said.

"So did most of the town. She was some kind of office junior at Springer's. The builder's merchants on Sheffield Road. You wanna know about her and who might really have topped her, you should talk to them."

On the whole, I was glad to get out of that house, and my next port of call was obvious.

According to the big, green sign outside their yard, Springer's Builder's Merchants were established in the mid-1940s, not long after the end of World War Two.

It was the largest unit on Sheffield Road Trading estate, a vast yard full of all the bits and pieces builders might need, and it was busy. Several men were working in different areas, some filling their vans with sacks of cement or lengths of wood or whatever, another crew loading their flatbed truck with packs of bricks banded together with metal straps. A dark-haired, youngish man in a brown, stockman's overall was wandering round the yard with another, bulkier man wearing navy blue overalls and rigger boots, and occasionally they would pause while overalls and rigger boots would point and speak (I couldn't hear what they were saying) and brown stockman would write on his clipboard. It seemed obvious to me that brown stockman was an employee, and overalls and rigger boots was a customer. Of course, it could be that the bigger man was the boss ordering the young chap to get the yard properly organised, but I didn't think so. Apart from anything else, the tan coloured rigger boots wouldn't really go with the black Mercedes parked in the slot marked 'Managing Director'.

There was plenty of parking space near the office block which was one side of the yard and when I pulled into a vacant spot, it gave me a good view of the back of a man's head in what looked like one of the smaller offices.

I stepped into the main reception, a sparkling clean area, where everything had that air of newness about it.

I was faced with a pretty forty-something tapping away slowly on her word processor. She was obviously not a professional typist. She deployed a 'hunt and peck' technique as if she had to look for every key. A younger woman, not much more than a girl really, had a headset on and was handling the telephone. Judging by the number of calls she was taking, I guessed that the builders of Haxford were getting ready for a glut of work come the summer.

"Good afternoon, madam," said forty-something, whose name, according to the little plaque on her desk was, Nancy Farmer. "How may I help you?"

I almost ordered a burger, fries, and Diet Coke, but I checked myself in time. "Christine Capper," I announced. "I'm a blogger, vlogger and radio presenter, and I'm looking into the murder of Rebecca Walmer."

Startled. That was the best way to describe her reaction. She matched it with her voice. "Becky?"

"Yes."

"Dear me. That's an awful long time ago."

"It is. Tell me, is there anyone still here who remembers her?"

"Yes. Me, and the boss, Mr Springer."

"Oh, good. Could you spare me a few minutes?"

"I – I'm not sure. I'm very busy."

You could have fooled me. I had to suppress that thought before it escaped my lips. I mean, if all she had to do was tap away at the keyboard at a snail's pace, she couldn't be that busy. Or maybe she was writing her autobiography while waiting for Mr Springer to order his afternoon vodka and dry martini. And talking of Mr Springer... "How about the boss, then?"

"Well, I'm not sure. He's quite—"

At that moment, brown stockman, still carrying

his clipboard, walked in, nodded an acknowledgement to the two women, knocked on the connecting door and without waiting for permission, entered the inner office, closing the door behind him.

"I'm sorry," Nancy Farmer apologised to me. "Now. You were saying?"

"I need to speak to someone who remembers Becky, and it really is important, Ms Farmer. I mean, it was one of the most shocking crimes this town has ever seen, and I'll be running a feature on it. I want to be sure to get my facts straight. So if you're too busy, how about I speak to your boss?"

"Well, he's busy, too, I mean… Oh, very well. I'll see if he can fit you in."

The change of heart came from one of my most determined stares, the kind which said, 'I'm Christine Capper. People don't say no to me'. She picked up her extension. After muttering into the mouthpiece, she put it down and spoke to me. "He'll be just a few minutes. Would you like to take a seat?"

She waved me to a comfortable bench by the entrance and I sat down.

While I waited, I watched her at the keyboard, and the change was dramatic. All of a sudden she was hitting those keys at a speed I could only envy. Was it my arrival? Or had she been waiting for a fresh coat of nail varnish to dry? Or perhaps she'd had a heavy night and she was running on empty. I had days like that, days when I really couldn't be bothered and applied the same hunt and peck technique she'd been using when I walked in.

I waited less than ten minutes before brown stockman came out of the office, Ms Farmer's extension buzzed and after speaking to (I assumed) the boss, she left her seat and ushered me into the inner sanctum.

A small room, I had a smashing view of my Fiat Diablo when I looked through the window over his shoulder.

Closer to home, Brian Springer was about as busy as Nancy Farmer had been. When he rose to shake hands, I glanced at his TFT monitor and he was in the middle of an online sudoku. He had quite a few of the different squares filled in, too. Did everyone at this place have too much time on their hands?

He was about fifty-ish, tall and good looking in a rugged, Haxford sort of way, but his suit could have done with some attention from an iron or a press if his wife wasn't of the ironing type. Slightly overweight, I noticed that although his tie was fastened snugly to the collar, the top button of his shirt was undone. The shirt collar was obviously no longer his size. Perhaps he couldn't afford a new shirt. Alternatively, perhaps he didn't care. Let's face it, most of the time, he would be dealing with builders and they were unlikely to be concerned with sartorial minutiae.

"Mrs Capper. Haxford's famous private eye."

"I'm sorry? I'm a vlogger and blogger and—"

"A radio presenter. I know. I was at Christmas Manor when your mystery hour was launched, and I remember that the police asked you to look into the killings until they could get there."

"You were at Christmas Manor?" If I sounded astonished, it's because I was. Most of the invited guests were from the travel and leisure industry.

"As a company, we supplied most of the materials for the reconstruction. You and I didn't speak. To be honest, we didn't even meet, but I was there – with my wife, naturally – and I was very impressed with your account of the Graveyard Poisoner case." He sat down again. "So what's this about Rebecca? It's a long time ago."

"Twenty years," I agreed sitting opposite him. "Frankly there's a rumour that the man convicted of the crime wasn't even in Haxford that night."

He smiled. "I should think that's a matter for the police."

"It is, but I'd like to get some background on Becky. For my vlog. I'm not investigating or anything." I could be quite skilled at lying when I wanted.

"It's a long time ago, and I really don't remember too much about her. A pretty girl, always cheerful, always had a smile on her face."

Standard, Haxford *don't speak ill of the dead*, and it was not what I wanted. "It has been suggested that she was, quite, er, flighty. How can I put it? Easy pickings for any young man."

"I really couldn't comment. It's not like I knew her that well. Of course, I was only the assistant manager back then. My grandfather founded the company in 1945, and my old man took over in the late sixties. Dad was still in control of the company at the time Becky worked for us."

Thank you for that brief, pointless, and totally

boring history lesson, I thought. Aloud, I asked, "So you don't know where she was or who she was with that night?"

His brow creased. "You're sure you're not on an official investigation, Mrs Capper?"

"Scouts honour." An idiotic thing to say. I was never in the Scouts. I couldn't be. I was female. Mind, I was never in the Girl Guides, either. Not even a Brownie.

"I'm working from memory," Springer told me, "but I think we were at Jumping Jacks."

"We? You were with her?"

He gave another easy laugh. "No, no. You misunderstand me. It was – correct me if I'm wrong – Easter weekend."

I agreed with a nod and carried on listening.

"As I recall, it was the night of our annual, staff Easter party. My parents were quite religious and even now, we always throw a party for the guys and gals every Christmas and Easter as a sort of thank you for the staff efforts, and it's always at Jumping Jacks."

What did his parents' religious inclinations have to do with a staff booze up, I wondered? I didn't ask. "Would it have been the Candlelight then?"

"No, no. I think we did use it when it was the Candlelight, but at the time we're talking about, Gus Leach had taken it over and renamed the place Jumping Jacks."

I shuddered at the mention of Gus Leach and memories of the case I was involved in, the one that almost prompted me to hand in my PI licence. In

42

order to bring us back on track, I asked, "You weren't with Becky on the night in question?"

Again with the laugh. "Dear me, no. I think Pauline, my wife, might have had something to say about that, don't you?"

I'm sure I would if it was Dennis, but Dennis didn't work with women, unless you counted Sandra Limpkin at the Snacky and he didn't really work with her. His interest only extended as far as the food she served and he wouldn't have anything else to do with her unless she owned a classic car instead of an old van.

"No, I spent the evening in the background with my wife, my mother, and father," Springer went on. "The old man never really approved of Jumping Jacks, and mother wasn't too fond of the place either. Still isn't, if it comes to that." Another false laugh. "Mind you, she's eighty-three years of age. Not really into gangsta-rap."

She was not on her own and I was thirty years younger than her.

"Your father's still with you?" I asked, just to be sociably nosy.

He shook his head. "Sadly not. He died three years ago. Eighty-four at the time. Not a bad innings." He changed the subject. "If you're really looking for background on Becky, Nancy, my PA, is the person to speak to. I don't say she and Becky were close friends, but they were around the same age, and as well as working with Becky, Nancy was at Jumping Jacks that night." A momentary pause. "I have to say, however, you're chasing rumours that are without foundation. As I recall, the police

43

had solid evidence against Jack Prater and when he was confronted with it, he confessed. Sending him to prison for life was the correct decision in my book."

I got to my feet and shook hands. "Thanks for your time, Mr Springer. Would you mind if I spoke to your PA now?"

"No. Of course not. Be my guest. Oh, and if you put this out on your vlog or on Radio Haxford, I'd appreciate a mention for the company."

"Count on it," I lied, and left him to his sudoku. I wouldn't even give Dennis a mention on the radio or my vlog, never mind a builders' merchant I knew nothing about. Besides, there was something about him I didn't like, something I didn't trust.

After some debate, Nancy Farmer led me through to a rest room at the rear of the reception area where she offered me a welcome cup of tea, which was an improvement on that I had been given at the Anguages' place. That wasn't saying much. Boiled vinegar with sour milk would have been better than tea with the Anguage family.

We made ourselves comfortable at a Formica topped table, and I went into my false routine.

"Do you mind if I speak frankly?" Nancy asked when I was through.

"I prefer it."

"Becky was a good worker. She came to us straight from school and she was always eager to learn, very competent, never late for work, and always willing to put in extra hours as and when she was needed."

"But?"

"But?"

I sipped tea. "Your opening words hinted there was something else about her."

"She was a little tart."

"Ah. I have heard whispers."

"Yes, well, this time I'm whispering because I don't want anyone else to hear." And with that she lowered her voice and leaned across the table, giving me a nostril full of Cheeky Charlie or some other cheap scent. "One afternoon, I caught her in one of the back sheds with a young builder. Her skirt was round her waist and knickers weren't where they were supposed to be, and neither were his underpants. You get my meaning?"

"Loud and clear," I agreed, although in truth, she was anything but loud and clear. She was still whispering.

"I gave her a good talking to, and she apologised, begged me not to tell Mr Irwin—"

"Irwin?"

"Irwin Springer. Mr Brian's father. He was still running the company then. Very upright, Mr Irwin was. He'd have sacked her on the spot."

I slotted all this information to the back of my mind, confident that I would remember it when I got home. "That's just one incident, though, Nancy," I pointed out.

"There were others. Not at work, but when we were on company nights out. Christmas, Easter and the like. On one do, she was seen on the back seat of a car with one of our warehouse hands giving her what for, and that night at Jumping Jacks, the night she was killed, she was all over several lads. Any one of them could have gone home with her before Jack Prater got to her."

"I see. And talking of Prater, did you see him at Jumping Jacks?"

She sniffed and shook her head. "I wouldn't have known him if I had."

Chapter Four

I came out of the building and climbed into the Diablo (Dennis was saying that now he was fully recovered, we didn't need such a large-ish vehicle) started the engine, and waited for it to warm up, and as I did so, I glanced at Springer's office where he was arguing with overalls and rigger boots, the man I had seen wandering round the yard with brown stockman's coat earlier. I say arguing. Springer was certainly animated, and the set of his jaw seemed to suggest annoyance. Was it down to my visit? Or did overalls and rigger boots have some grievance? Whatever the background, it told me that I was right when I elected not to trust Springer. He was obviously a bit of a snapper.

I took out my phone, set the camera on video and as surreptitiously as I could, I panned it round the yard for about thirty seconds and then focussed on Springer's office. If there was something wrong, something to do with Becky Walmer, I wanted evidence, scant as it may be. In any case, even if their argument was nothing to do with me or Becky, the video would give me something I could use on my vlog if I ever decided on a piece about the construction industry in Haxford.

Once done, I drove away, my mind pondering

the last half hour or so.

Nothing of Wynn Anguage and Nancy Farmer's opinion of Becky had ever been revealed in the press or online, which was hardly surprising. The phrase 'never speak ill of the dead' rang through my mind yet again. If Nancy's story was true, then it was possible that Becky's murder had a sexual motive rather than the popular but staid view of disturbing Prater at his nefarious work. To my knowledge, Prater had never molested any of his female victims.

I couldn't decide where I should go next. Logic dictated that I should speak to George and Andrea Walmer, Becky's parents, but I guessed that even twenty years on it would be reopening an old wound. It would be like me recalling the attack on Dennis, the major difference being that Dennis survived the attack on him. Besides, I wasn't sure what they might be able to tell me. They were in Mablethorpe the night it happened. In addition, I doubted that the Walmers would thank me for calling into question their deceased daughter's reputation, especially when I didn't know if her lack of morality had any bearing on her murder.

Once home, I don't know how long I sat in the car trying to decide what to do. A number of options crossed my mind, amongst which was to take the video to Mandy and leave it with her, and/or make arrangements to see Prater in HMP Wakefield, neither of which appealed. Then I remembered that before the email, text, and call, I was busy roughing out an account of the McCrudden affair, so I decided that my best course of action was to get on with it. Eric and the Radio Haxford troops were due the following day and if I could have it finished, I could hand it over to…

My thoughts ground to a halt. Eric. Didn't he say Christine Capper's Mystery Hour needed a change of direction? And as an experienced radio producer/director he might be able to see the best way forward.

I dug out my smartphone and hesitated with my fingers hovering over the on-screen keypad.

The Allbrook case cropped up at the beginning of March, and in the middle of it, we were in Cambridge for my niece's wedding. That week involved two separate, unconnected killings, neither of them intentional (in my opinion) and I was so incensed at the eventual outcome that I put the idea of investigative campaigning to Eric. I don't know why. It's not like I was some kind of hardline activist, and Eric was still thinking about it when my enthusiasm petered out, but at the time, I'd never been so fired up.

Now, here I was again, getting on my soapbox, ready to fight but this time it was on the thinnest of evidence; the say so of a man who was a career criminal, the courtroom insistence of a man who had subsequently spent twenty years prison, the questionable testimony of has partner, and an iffy (illegal?) video from someone I assumed to be a police officer. Even if I had confirmed the sender's status right, how did I know that the officer in question was not a friend or on the payroll of organised crooks like Prater and Tyndall? I didn't.

In fact, when I thought more about it, all I had

were hints and suspicions of a miscarriage of justice, and if I put it to Eric, he would be guarded to say the least.

On the other hand, maybe it was time to show everyone just what I was made of. I was Christine Capper, Capper the Copper, the only licenced private eye in Haxford, a radio star, a woman who preferred to kick sleeping dogs in the backside rather than letting them laze around on the front room rug all day.

I hit the key and rang, only to be connected to Eric's voicemail. Typical. He was probably in a meeting with the big boss.

"Eric, it's Chrissy. I've something I need to talk to you about. Could you call me back please? If it's difficult, don't worry. I'll catch you at my place tomorrow."

That last part was flannel. The last thing I wanted was to wait.

Once in the house, making a desperate attempt to calm down, I spent half an hour in front of the wardrobe mirror trying on, first the sweater, which was not only gorgeous and luxurious, but warm enough to dispel the chilly days, cool enough to welcome the sunshine. A snip at thirty pounds, but I wouldn't tell Dennis that. To him thirty pounds was what he would make changing a wheel for a motorist who couldn't or couldn't be bothered doing it him/herself.

Happy with the jumper, I closed the curtains and tried on the underwear. Snug and cool. I'm saying no more than that.

I was in the front room enjoying a cup of tea

with Cappy the Cat for company (which meant no company at all) when Eric rang back at four o'clock.

"The Mystery Hour," I announced. "You said you were looking for a new direction."

"I did, and I am, and it needs to happen fairly quickly, Chrissy. I've just come from a meeting with the big boss—" (Didn't I tell you that's where he'd be?) "—and after last week's rating returns, he's talking of pulling the plug anytime now, and getting you to anchor at least one music programme."

"No chance. I'm not a DJ. If that's what he's threatening, I'll cut out and see my solicitor."

"You mean your brother."

"Stephen is still a solicitor and perfectly familiar with contract law. The boss can't turn me into something I'm not. Anyway, I've had an idea. It's a case which has just dropped on me today. I can't really talk at length over the phone. Can you spare me some time tomorrow after we're through with the recording?"

"Of course. Give me a flavour."

"Cold case and a possible miscarriage of justice."

I could hear the smile in his voice. "I like the sound of that." There was a momentary pause. "Local to Haxford?"

"One of the most shocking murders the town has ever seen, but the man serving life for it might just be innocent. I stress 'might'."

"Oh, my word. I'm on a pleasure overload already. I assume the police are looking into it."

The phone gave a beep so loud that it was

51

painful. I checked the screen. An incoming text message. Ignoring it, I replied to Eric's query. "No police. Not yet, anyway, but it won't be long so if we want it on air, we'll have to move quickly."

"Great. I'll speak to you tomorrow then, either before we get the recording under way or after we're finished. All right?"

He rang off and I opened the text message. Short and sweet, it read, *Good on you* and it came from the same unidentified number as the text and call earlier in the day.

It would be tempting to ask how he knew I'd made a start on the inquiry, but the answer to that was too easy. He had to be a police officer, and after I spoke to Mandy, she told Paddy Quinn, who reported to his boss, and somewhere along the line, someone contacted this man's superiors, probably high ups in the Met. They would have disseminated the message to the various teams, and he was amongst that hoi-polloi. The police service could move like lightning when it wanted, especially when its reputation might be at stake.

With that knowledge, I archived both texts, then booted up my laptop and archived the email and its damning video. If the police came asking, I would have to tell them all I knew, but without documentary evidence from the phone or the machine (at least not until they searched for it) they would be hard pressed to track down the whistleblowing officer through me.

As I had already realised outside Springer's office, I was short of solid information, not only about Becky's murder but mostly about Jack Prater.

I knew of him. Everyone at Haxford police station did, but I didn't actually know him. It did occur to me that he was about Dennis's age. A year or two his junior, to be accurate. So did my old man know more?

Discretion was the major problem when asking Dennis anything. His interpretation of the word was fitting a new wiper motor to a car when the customer only wanted a wiper blade. Dennis would fit the motor *at his discretion* and he could always think up some complex technobabble to explain it (and the bill) away. When it came to keeping things quiet and confidential, he couldn't. He had a mouth as wide as the Humber estuary.

Still, when you're begging, you can't be choosy, so the moment he got home and we settled down to our evening meal, I told him of my day, starting with the bad news from Eric.

Working his way quickly through a defrosted and microwaved steak and ale pie, he was also eyeing up the classifieds in the Haxford Recorder when I said, "Radio Haxford are talking about shutting down the mystery hour."

"I don't believe it."

His reaction encouraged me until I realised he was still reading the paper.

"There's a bloke here asking four hundred quid for a 1965 Morris Minor."

"You shouldn't read at the dinner table, Dennis," I told him. "It's bad manners."

"I wonder how much work it needs doing."

I slipped into irritated mode. "Dennis, I'm speaking to you."

My presence finally clicked. "What? What do you want?"

"I said, Radio Haxford are talking about dropping the mystery hour. It's turned into a bit of a flop."

"Well, I never thought it would come to much." He glanced at the newspaper again. "I wonder if he's had—"

"Will you shut up about the 1964 Morris and listen to me?"

"1965."

"I don't care if it's 1965 or 1695. For someone who never thought the mystery hour would amount to much, you were the one spending the fizzing fortune I would make from Radio Haxford before I even signed the contract."

He put down his knife and fork, moved the paper from under his elbow, and concentrated on me. "One, you have a contract, and if they're dropping you, they have to pay you. And two, they didn't make Morris Minors in sixteen whenever. They didn't have internal combustion engines. They didn't start making them until—"

"I don't care." I hissed out a sigh and gathered my thoughts. "I have another problem. Becky Walmer."

"Never heard of him."

"Her. She is a her, not a him. Well, she was. She was murdered about twenty years ago. A man named Jack Prater got life for it. I just wondered if you knew him."

Returning to his meal, he chewed on a mouthful of pie and mashed potato and looked around the

54

room. "Prater... Prater... Prater... I don't suppose you know what kind of motor he drove?"

"Maybe it was a 1695 Morris. I don't know, Dennis, and it doesn't matter. Did you know him?"

"Can't say as how... Hang on. Didn't he strangle some lass off Sheffield Road?"

"I just said so. Becky Walmer."

"Ah, right, well, he'd be a couple of years younger than me, but I think Geronimo knew him from school. He's your best bet. Geronimo."

Geronimo was Tony Wharrier, Dennis's senior partner at Haxford Fixers, and the moment I finished my meal, I moved to the front room and rang him at home, only to learn that he was taking his wife, Val, out for a meal.

"I do remember Prater but I barely knew him. He was at least a year, maybe two behind me at school. Anyway, I'm sorry, Christine, but I can't talk right now. We're ready for going out. Could you catch up with me tomorrow at the workshop and in the meantime, I'll give the memory cells a workout?"

"Not tomorrow, Tony. It's my day for recording my radio shows and I won't be finished until well into the afternoon. How about first thing Thursday?"

"Fine. Yes. Thursday morning, then."

I returned to the kitchen to find Dennis, who had finished his meal, cutting off his mobile.

"Tony's taking Val out to dinner," I reported, "so I'll catch him on Thursday at your place."

"Sad, that."

"What? Tony taking his wife out to dinner? Maybe you should try it sometime."

"This dumbo let that Morris go for three hundred and fifty sovs. I told him, I said, I'd have happen gone to five for it."

"Will you shut up about the Morris manky Minor. And since the mystery hour is on the point of being dumped, we don't have five hundred pounds to spare."

"All right, all right. Get the knot out of your knickers. You're coming to our place tomorrow, did you say?"

"Actually, I said Thursday and you can pay for my breakfast at Sandra's Snacky."

I don't know whether it was the Morris Minor 1000 which had gone or threatening to hit Dennis where it hurt (i.e. in the wallet) but whatever the cause, the argument ended when he stomped from the room.

Chapter Five

My fickle neighbours on Bracken Close entertained an ambivalent attitude to my radio fame. It was excellent for scoring brownie points at dinner parties. "Christine Capper lives across the street, you know. She's a radio star." It was not so great when the team turned up every Wednesday with their big van, unloaded all their paraphernalia into the house, and then ran generators all day to power the equipment. "Can you please ask them to keep the noise down?"

Not likely. The only way they could do that would be to leave the stuff permanently in my conservatory which I wouldn't entertain, and there was no way of silencing the generators other than plugging their hi-tech apparatus into my mains electricity and our power bills were big enough, thank you.

During the winter months, the soundproof, squeak-proof booth I sat in for recording my programmes kept me nice and warm but I was the only one in the house who was comfortable. The crew often complained that the house was cold. It would be. It was the same argument as the generators. I refused to turn on the central heating while they were in residence because they were forever opening the conservatory door to go out to their vehicles for bits and pieces.

With the weather warming up, that booth, which they put together during the set-up became the equivalent of a steaming sauna. I needed more frequent breaks for cold drinks, and inevitably that slowed down the recording process.

Even on a good day, it was rare that the crew got away much before half past two in the afternoon. On those good days, if I didn't make too many goofs reading through the scripts, if there weren't too many gremlins in the equipment, if there were not too many instances of Cappy the Cat chasing the various cables around the floor and often ripping them out of their sockets, we could have everything recorded by half past twelve, one o'clock, after which they would tear everything apart and be gone an hour and a half later.

On a bad day, they could be there until four o'clock or even later, which put me under extra pressure to get everything ready for our evening meal... mine and Dennis's (and Cappy the Cat's) I mean, not mine and the Radio Haxford team. They cost me enough in brews and biscuits without inviting them for tea. (Note to my hupper clarse readers: it may offend your finer sensibilities, but we common Haxforders, by whom I mean Dennis and me, not the likes of Barbara and Fred Timmins, always called our evening meal 'tea', not 'dinner'.)

On Wednesday, April 26, I was in an inconsistent frame of mind. It had not stopped raining all night and although I had a large welcome mat inside the conservatory door, it was wasted on the Radio Haxford people. By mid-morning, the creamy coloured laminate floor looked like it hadn't seen a mop since the previous summer. The police forensic people would have been in seventh heaven taking pictures of the muddy footprints, and aside from sheer frustration at the cleaning ahead of me, my biggest puzzle was where they pick up the mud? Getting their gear into the house, they didn't need to touch the gardens front or back.

When Eric first put the Mystery Hour prospect to me, I was (secretly) over the moon, although I did feel more than a tremor of trepidation at the potential of a whole new career in entertainment. The audience reaction declined during the first month of the year and according to the grapevine, the big boss was dropping ever stronger hints that it would soon have to make way for something more in keeping with audience expectations. Grapevine nothing. Hadn't Eric been telling me for weeks now that we were in the tumbrel on our way to an appointment with Madame Guillotine, and hadn't he said just the previous day that our execution was imminent?

Not only were they threatening my rosy, cosy life, but it was hard work. I was the one who had to get everything right when we were recording. I wasn't allowed to stumble over my words, and if I got a name wrong, I had to do it again and again and again until it was right. Alden Upley, who ran the public library, was a case in point. I don't know how many times I referred to him as Alderman Upley in those early days.

My mood did not improve as the morning

progressed and I knew what was behind it: the twin problems of the inevitable and impending demise of Christine Capper's Mystery Hour and whether Jack Prater's potential innocence would be enough to stave it off.

Still and all, we were done by two o'clock but I stayed in the booth to keep warm, and watched Eric discussing the output with our new sound man, Tom Nixon. If Tom gave it the thumbs up, we were through for the day and I could leave them to dismantle the gear while I went back to lounging around the front room with Cappy the Cat for company... which is as good as saying I would be on my own until Dennis got home about half past six.

Tom had signed on in the New Year and he was spared the attentions of Eric's daughter, Olivia, on two fronts. One, he was in his late fifties, a good thirty-odd years older than her, and two, he was married with a son also older than her. This is not to say that Olivia would be interested in him anyway, but she did have a bit of a thing going with our previous sound engineer, Tim. Admittedly, the memories were fresh enough for her to get Tom's name mixed up. I'd heard her call him Tim Dickson on more than one occasion, but that was hardly surprising. She still referred to me as Pristine Clapper now and then, and I'd been telling her for the last nine months that it's Christine Capper. But that's Olivia. I wouldn't say she's a thickhead. That would be an insult to all the thickheads of this world.

Tom was not the man with the final say. That

was Eric's prerogative, but he made his decision on advice from the technicians around him. If one of them had doubts, then we re-recorded whatever was wrong. Of all the experts, Tom was the most important. There's a difference between recording a message on your webcam for Aunt Lulu's 101st birthday, and recording an entire programme for broadcast on local radio, and I don't mean in the detail of the actual message. If we want to be technical, my Aunt Lulu *was* born 101 years ago, but she'd been dead for the last twenty years, so the detail of such a message would be pointless anyway.

No, I'm talking quality. It had to be spot on. No extraneous noises like Cappy the Cat squawking at the birds in the back garden, no irritating phone calls in the middle of a session (I recalled a text arriving in the middle of the session during the week I got involved in the Allbrook/Keogh affair) and no questionable microphones, i.e. those likely to break down.

Extraneous noises were fairly easy to eliminate. It's why they sat me on a squeak-proof chair in a soundproofed booth. Tricky, dicky equipment was strictly their problem, not mine, other than the way in which it might impinge on the time taken to get the job done.

As I watched, Tom talked, Eric nodded judiciously, asked a couple of questions, Tom replied, and Eric ended the conversation with a nod of thanks, turned to face me, and gave me the thumbs up.

That was the cue for me to leave my temporary cubbyhole, move to the kitchen, make myself a cup of tea before the motley descended on my kettle, after which I made my way to the front room, switched on our electric convector heater, curled my feet up on the large settee, and made myself comfortable in the fire's warmth.

I was tempted to switch on the TV, but there were two problems with that. First, I didn't care for daytime TV (I wasn't that keen on evening TV, come to that) and second, I'd need the volume turned up to painful levels to hear it over the cacophony of men and women dismantling and removing the bits and pieces from the conservatory. Cappy the Cat obviously agreed with me to judge from the way he trotted into the living room, hopped onto the settee, deliberately brushed against my leg in a gesture which asked, 'is it time for a feed yet' and then snuggled down near my feet when I refused to move.

Once the team were packed and ready for leaving, Eric traditionally popped his head into the living room to say 'au revoir' but as per our agreement on the phone the previous evening he deviated this time.

"We're finished, Chrissy. The crew are just having a brew and they'll be on their way. You wanted a word?"

"It's just an idea."

"I'm listening."

And now I hesitated, trying to decide where to begin.

The silence was broken by his daughter, who popped in to deliver a beaker of tea for him. "Oh, I'm sorry, Mrs Cropper. I forgot about you. Did you want some tea?"

"No thank you, Olivia. I'm all teed up and mostly teed off. And by the way, it's Capper."

Eric smiled as she disappeared. "She'll get your name right one day."

"I'll look forward to it." What was left of my tea had gone cold, and I wish I'd asked Olivia to bring me a fresh beaker. I made an effort to put my grumbling thoughts to one side. "A man named Jack Prater. He's serving a life sentence. Been in prison for twenty years and he could be innocent. I stress could be."

He took a sip from the beaker and grimaced. Olivia never did make a decent cuppa.

"I mentioned it to Sir yesterday after you rang, and because I couldn't give him any details, he said he might be interested, I stress, might be."

'Sir' was another euphemism for the big boss, whose name was never mentioned. I wasn't sure I knew it. It was something like Longjohn, but he preferred never to be mentioned, and that was likely a means of ducking the flak for shows like Christine Capper's Mystery Hour. If no one talked about the big boss, then Eric would be blamed.

Eric was still talking. "Chasing up a potential miscarriage of justice sounds like a good idea, but do remember, Chrissy, we're an entertainment channel, not news, not documentary, and not campaigners. But before we commit ourselves, why don't you tell me everything you know, everything you learned yesterday, and we'll take it from there."

So I did. Over the next twenty minutes or half an hour, after showing him the video, I gave him a

63

blow by blow account of my previous day from the moment the email arrived until I left Nancy Farmer at Springer's. I stopped short of the discussion between Dennis and me because it didn't make much sense, but I did tell him that I had a contact (no names no pack drill at this stage) who knew Prater back in his school days.

"I'll be speaking to him... or her tomorrow morning," I concluded.

Eric didn't answer right away. He took a gulp of tea, grimaced yet again, and then called for Olivia, asking her to bring more tea, and I asked her to make a cup for me, too.

"Very good, Mrs Trapper."

Trapper? That was a new one and it was getting a little too close to crapper for my liking. "Olivia, luv, it's Capper. C-A-P-P-E-R. As in a hat. All right?"

She giggled. "Sorry, Mrs Hatter."

Will I ever learn to keep my big mouth shut?

Determined to wipe the smirk from her father's face, I focussed on him. "So what do you think?"

He didn't answer right away, and I read the signs. He had something to say and he was calculating the best way of saying it.

"Eric?"

"Yes. I'll tell you what I think, Christine."

Suddenly I was no longer Chrissy but Christine. I wasn't going to like this.

"I've seen a remarkable change come over you ever since your niece's wedding in – where was it? – Oxford? Cambridge?"

He knew perfectly well where it was.

64

"Cambridge," I confirmed. "I've changed? I don't think so? I'm still the home-loving and friendly, Haxford girl I always was. I take care of my husband and family, and my cat, I'm looking forward to the coronation the week after next, and I'm planning a holiday for Dennis and me. That is me. Christine Capper. The same easy-going woman you've known for the last year or so."

"I beg to differ. You're more confident, more strident, more determined. You even hover on the edge of – I hesitate to use the word – pushy. You're also more prone to get bees in your bonnet. You did over the Allbrook Farm-slash-Keogh business, and from all you told me, you refused to let go at Gaven Hall. Don't get me wrong. It's not a bad thing. The major asset any performer needs, whether on radio, TV or live, is self-belief and you seem to have more of it these days. You leave the stage fright behind the moment you get behind the microphone and from that moment, Christine Capper is in control."

Was all this true? I didn't think so, especially considering the number of gaffes I made during the recording. But if it was… "You can blame Radio Haxford for that. I've come a long way in the last twelve months."

Olivia returned and handed us a beaker each. As she left, I took a mouthful of tea and scowled. The idiot girl had put sugar in it and she knew I took saccharin not sugar.

He took a swallow of tea and scowled. "Tastes like saccharin."

His numbskull daughter again. We swapped beakers, and settled with the correct brews, Eric went on.

"You have, indeed, come an awful long way from the nervous woman who sat with Reggie when you took over the agony aunt spot from Lizzie Finister, but you're still quite inexperienced, and your – again I hesitate to use the word – gung-ho approach needs to be tempered to the demands of a local radio station. We can't just dive headlong into, er, issues."

I was about to protest but he held up his hands to stop me.

"Yes, yes, I know, I said Christine Capper's Mystery Hour needs to change, but think about the outcome of the Allbrook affair and the Gaven Hall case. You were fired up, outraged on both counts, and I didn't agree with you. People died, Christine, and there had to be punishment, but you didn't see it that way."

This time I managed to get my complaint in. "Yes I did. I just objected to custodial sentences."

"And again, I have to disagree. But these are personal opinions and they count for nothing. What I'm saying is, don't let your personal bias get in the way of your professional work. I'm sure you don't allow it in your role as private investigator, and you shouldn't let it influence you in your radio work or you'll come out as some kind of self-obsessed celebrity, a woman to whom nothing matters except herself."

Pushy? Gung-ho? Celebrity? That last was the ultimate insult as far as I was concerned. Thanks to my popular blog/vlog, I'd always been a minor, tiny, tiny, celebrity in Haxford, and of course many people knew me from days in the police, and I often basked in the reflected glory of Dennis's renown as a mechanic. But to categorise me with all those mouthy wannabes from tripe TV like BB, BGT, TXF… well, it was just beyond the pale.

I needed to think about his words before I could properly respond, so I shifted the argument off to one side. "Fine As long as we both know where we stand."

"I'm not attacking you, Chrissy. I'm trying to educate you."

At least I was Chrissy again. "So what about the Prater case?"

He didn't hesitate. "Tell me where I go wrong, but you still have contacts in the police, don't you? People like Mandy Hiscoe and Paddy Quinn?"

"Yes."

"And the chances are this Prater business will impinge on the reputation of one of their colleagues… if it's true, that is."

"It's a debate I've already had with Mandy. What matters to me is Prater's guilt or innocence."

"Quite so." He took a wet from the correct beaker this time. "I spent a good few years working for the BBC and as it happens, I know Henry Fairburn, so here's what I propose. I'll try to get a word with him tonight and see what he can tell us about his alleged break-in. It may not be much. As a private investigator, what else would you recommend?"

"A chat with Becky's parents, and a prison visit. We need to see Jack Prater and see what he has to say. He confessed. If he later withdrew that confession but couldn't back up his claim of duress, maybe twenty years inside has loosened his tongue." I smiled. "Especially when he learns of Tyndall's interview with Scotland Yard."

Chapter Six

Nobody could mistake the premises of Haxford Fixers. Situated on the ground floor of Haxford Mill, along the canal side, the sign was almost invisible beneath the muck covering it, but the wrecker and the van bore their name, and if that wasn't enough to guide you, there were always several cars and vans and small trucks parked outside waiting for the attention of Dennis and his three partners.

When I walked in at half past nine on Thursday morning, the view was a familiar one. All I could see of Dennis were his legs and his bottom – in overalls, naturally. But you didn't think I meant... did you? Dennis was a mechanic, not a builder. He could never be that bare-cheeked.

We had a contemplative Wednesday evening. While he sat watching his regular repeats of *Top Gear* or *Bangers & Cash*, frequently grumbling about the things the presenters did and didn't know, I sat in the conservatory watching the rainy, April sky darken until half past eight, and then having turned the vertical blinds, I sat in the soft glow of the lighting, effectively staring into space.

But I wasn't simply gazing at the walls. Everything kept running on through my jumbled mind: Jack Prater, Becky Walmer, Nancy Farmer, Brian Springer, Mandy, Paddy, Tyndall and the two Scotland Yard detectives, the things Eric had said to me. Especially the things Eric said to me.

Pushy? Gung-ho? Me? We Haxforders are true Yorkshire folk. We never beat about the bush. We just get it said and if you don't like what you're hearing, well that's tough because that's how we are.

Except that I was not like that and never had been. The word tact was missing from Dennis's dictionary (as it was for most Haxforders) but although I was a true daughter of the White Rose, I had always been careful to ensure that I did not hurt people with my words. Other than when I was angry, that is.

How dare Eric Reitman compare me to some loudmouthed celeb?

I would have brought it up with Dennis, but he was still in a mood over having missed out on that Morris Minor a couple of nights back, and I knew what kind of response I'd get. It would just lead to another argument, so I kept quiet, and instead debated it with myself.

It was true to say that I was angered by the outcome of both the Gaven Hall and Allbrook Farm cases, and that annoyance led me into conflict with Mandy and Paddy in Haxford, and DCI Rothman in Cambridge. I won't go into detail. They're spelled out in another of my casebooks (A Call to Murder if you're really nosy like me).

Casting my mind back over the last twelve months, I detected the change Eric had mentioned in my approach to different cases. In the Wool Fair business, I had to come on strong with the victim's family, and in the McCrudden blackmail case, I lost the plot totally after Dennis was beaten up. But the Leach affair? So I came on strong but the subject of infidelity had always done that to me. And at Christmas Manor, the attitude of two men, both of whom looked down on me, rattled me to the point of retaliation.

Thinking deeper about it, the subtle but significant changes did begin with the McCrudden case, and that coincided with the sacking of Lizzie Finister and my appointment as the Radio Haxford agony aunt: the birth of my radio career. During that investigation I even outfaced the man who would eventually win the Haxford parliamentary seat.

Was it true? Was I turning into some arrogant, publicity-seeking, wannabe social media influencer ready to rant at the world because someone had commented on the size of my bust?

I took these thoughts to bed and a disturbed night and the dour prospect of a visit to Haxford Fixers for Thursday morning.

When I walked into the workshop, Dennis was bent under the hood of a Ford Focus (which was how come all I could see of him was his bottom half) tinkering with the engine or gearbox or something, and amongst the general background of noise, part of which was Reggie Monk's morning show coming through the radio, I could hear him muttering to the accompaniment of his spanners tapping away. Alongside that car, Greg Vetch was in the pit under an old Volvo doing whatever they did in the pit under an old Volvo. Beyond them, Lester Grimes was at his bench faffing with a curious looking, tiny box-type affair with a mass of wiring and cables coming out of it. From the paint shop next door, I could hear Tony Wharrier's spray gun at work.

No one registered my arrival until I cleared my throat and Lester looked round.

"Hey up, it's cuddly Chrissy. What's up, luv? Looking for a special feller whose thoughts might be turning to a summer of love. We can leave Cappy messing about with cars?"

"Thank you, Lester. Don't call me. I'll call you, but don't hold your breath."

It was a standard greeting between the two of us, and the exchange caused Dennis to emerge form under the bonnet of the Ford, straighten up and scowl at me. "What do you want?"

"A better attitude from you for a start off."

Greg's oil-stained face appeared from under the Volvo. "My fault, Chrissy. I've upset him."

I smiled. "What have you done, Greg?"

It was Dennis who answered. "Ask me who bought a sixty-five Morris Minor 1000 for three hundred and fifty dabs."

Greg chuckled. "If I don't double or treble me money, there's summat wrong with me."

"Good for you, Greg." I applauded him before turning on my husband. "If I hear much more about this Morris, I'll sign you up for a course in Morris dancing. And I'm here for breakfast, which you're paying for. Remember? I did tell you on Tuesday and again this morning before you left for work.

And I'm also here to see Tony."

While Dennis sulked, Lester leaned back in his seat and raised his voice to painful levels. "Geronimo, there's a cracking bit of skirt here to see you."

I appreciated Lester alerting Tony but I didn't care for being described in such a derogatory manner, and I warned him, "If you call me a cracking bit of skirt again, I'll crack your head open."

"And search for his brain?" Tony asked as he appeared from the paint shop. "Good morning, Christine. Could you wait about ten minutes? I just want to finish spraying this door."

I assumed he meant the door of a car and not the sliding door separating the workshop from the paint shop, so I agreed. He had always been more polite than any of his colleagues. "Of course, Tony. I'll be up in the Snacky with Dennis."

Dennis piped up right away. "Yeah but, I'm busy and—"

I cut my husband off by talking directly to Tony. "Dennis and I will be in the Snacky."

"Nice to see who's the boss, Cappy," Greg called from beneath the Volvo.

"Take note, Herriot. I'm a hen-pecked husband," Dennis replied.

We left the workshop, and walked to the front of the mill where we would take the service lift up to the third floor. "How does Greg react to being called Herriot?"

"He don't mind. Better'n Good Boy anyway."

Nickames were endemic to Haxford, and they

had struggled to find one for Greg. Originally they called him Good Boy on the slender grounds that his surname sounded like 'fetch' and if you threw a stick for a dog, you always patted it on the head and said, "Good boy," when it fetched the stick.

Dennis outlined the change (not for the first time) as we entered the lift. "It were Grimy's doing. He said Vetch sounded like 'vet', so we called him Herriot on account of how Johnny Herriot was a vet."

I knew there'd be an explanation. Stupid and childish, yes, but it's what I'd come to expect from Dennis and his partners. And it was typical of him to get part of it wrong. "James Herriot," I said.

"Johnny, James, who cares?"

"Mr Herriot, I would imagine."

"And Mrs Herriot if she was owt like you."

Most of the space on the third and the top floor was taken up by Sandra's Snacky, run by Sandra Limpkin, another old friend, as much of Dennis's as mine. She catered for all the small businesses in the building and their customers, and it was a standard port of call for Dennis and his pals every morning and lunchtime.

Sandra, a loud and outspoken woman of about fifty, was not in evidence, however. Instead, it was her daughter, Ursula, who took Dennis's order for a full English breakfast, and put on two slices of white toast and marmalade for me.

"Where's your mam, Ursula?" I asked as I collected our beakers of tea.

"Benidorm," she replied. "Some kind of early break with members of the over-50s club."

That was puzzling. "I didn't know she'd turned fifty."

"She hasn't. Not yet anyway. She's fifty in the summer."

"Then how did she—"

Ursula cut me off. "She lied about her age."

Obviously feeling a bit left out, Dennis threw in the inevitable comment with a telling glance at me. "Most women knock a few years off when they lie about their age."

"That's what I said," Ursula replied, "But apparently these over fifties get some good discounts on their holidays and nobody seemed to care."

I gave my other half an amused glance. "Maybe you should join, Dennis. I can't. I'm far too young."

We made our way to a table on the outer edge of the seating, and while we waited for the food to arrive, Dennis asked, "So what's this all about? I meanersay, you don't normally turn up here, especially when you're not working on summat."

I sighed. "You know, Dennis, ours has been a good marriage, but it could improve some if you listened to me."

"We're a pair together then, aren't we? You never listen to me."

I tutted. "I told you all about this the night before last."

"Yeah, but I've slept since then, haven't I?"

"Jack Prater," I reminded him.

"Oh, him? He's inside, where he belongs. Good riddance to bad rubbish. That's what I say."

"It's not what you said the other night. You said

you barely remember him."

"I don't, but I remember reading the papers when he topped that young lass. Cos he did, didn't he? Yes, and he's doing life for it, isn't he? Serves him right. He got what he deserved, killing a young girl like that."

"And what if he's innocent?"

"He isn't, though. He was found guilty, and the word is he owned up to it. And you should know. You were a copper then."

"No, Dennis. I'd left the force by that time."

"Had you? Oh. Right. Even so, there was that mate of yours? Wrigley. She was still on the force."

I knew right away who he was talking about. "You mean Risley. Linda Risley."

"That's him."

Linda was a detective constable when I was a police officer and she and I were good friends. What's more, she worked on the Becky Walmer case alongside Kitson and Penning. Her name hadn't occurred to me until Dennis mentioned it, and if anyone could throw any light upon Kitson's interrogation of Prater, it would be her.

Or could she?

For an offence as serious as murder, procedure would demand an inspector or above and during interrogation, he would invariably work with a fellow inspector or at worst a sergeant. He would not take a DC into a murder interview. Within a year or two of the Walmer case, Linda left the service and the last I heard she was working security in a shopping mall on the outskirts of Huddersfield.

Digging out my smartphone, I sourced the

number of the mall's management, and as our food arrived, I was talking to them. Typically, they refused to give me Linda's number but agreed that she still worked there and they would pass on a message asking her to ring me.

Dennis was not remotely troubled by my making the call. He was too busy wolfing down his breakfast. He ate so fast that it was as if he was terrified someone might come in and steal the food from under his knife and fork.

As I ended the call and concentrated on my toast, Tony walked in, went to the counter, ordered breakfast, and then joined us.

"How are you, Christine?"

"Can't complain, Tony… well, I could but it wouldn't get me anywhere. Are you okay, Val and the boys? Looking forward to the coronation?"

"We're fine, and as regards the latter point, I'll probably be working."

"Me too," Dennis grumbled.

Tony's features darkened and he came to the point. "Jack Prater. You do know he's in prison? Serving life, so Val told me. Murdered a young girl named Rebecca—"

"Walmer," I interrupted. "Yes, I know. But we've heard whispers that he might not have done it."

"Twaddle," Dennis declared. He pushed his empty plate to one side and picked up his mug of tea. "He admitted it."

"So my other half said," Tony commented as Ursula delivered his breakfast. Unlike Dennis, he opted for a bacon and egg sandwich to go with his tea. "Val looked it up after you rang the other night. I don't actually recall any of the details, but I do remember him from school. Cocky little snot, he was. Always getting into fights and couldn't keep his hands off other people's property." He bit off a large mouthful of sandwich and chewed on it.

I allowed him the silence for a moment, then asked. "You won't be surprised to learn that he was a seasoned burglar, then?"

"Not in the slightest. As I remember, he was a bad lot. And as for killing that girl, well, the story Val picked up on the web was that she disturbed him ransacking the house."

"The same tale I read. I spoke to his, er, partner, common-law wife, call her what you will, yesterday, and she insists he's innocent."

"Elaine Anguage," Tony said through another mouthful of his sandwich. "Yes, well, I certainly know her. Same age as me, same year at school. She has two children, presumably, Prater's, although there are no guarantees on that. Terrible woman. Even as a schoolgirl, she was anyone's for a bottle of cider and packet of cigarettes." He looked shocked. "I beg your pardon, Christine. I shouldn't be saying—"

"It's all right, Tony. We're all adults."

"I know Elaine," Dennis chipped in. "Her company never came free of charge, if you know what I mean."

While Tony finished off his sandwich, I cast my husband a meaningful stare. "And how would you know?"

"Everyone knew her, Christine," Tony cut in

78

before I could put Dennis on the spot about his life before me. "I'm surprised you don't know her. You were a police officer after all, and she was, er, active when you were on the force."

"After thirty years with Dennis, you forget such trivia," I pointed out. Tony grinned, Dennis scowled. I knew he wouldn't see the funny side of that remark. "I don't see what bearing Elaine's profession – for want of a better description – has on Prater's potential guilt."

"Well, you said she was insistent on his innocence. The police won't have taken much notice of her given her past record."

"Lying is part of her makeup," Dennis said.

I made a mental note of the trivia I had learned and decided I was running out of questions. The entire interlude had been a waste of time, although I did get my breakfast toast out of it.

"Do either of you know Becky's parents? Mrs and Mrs Walmer?"

Both shook their heads. "Older'n us by a good few years," Dennis said. "Live somewhere off Sheffield Road, I think. Getting on for Moor Top way. I don't wanna tell you how to do your job, our lass, but I shouldn't have thought they'd wanna help spring Jack Prater."

It didn't surprise me that Dennis denied knowing them, yet could tell me where they lived and how they were older than any of us. He had probably serviced their car sometime in the past.

"Thing is, Dennis, if Jack Prater really is innocent, then whoever killed Becky is still out there."

My husband shook his head. "If Jack Prater is innocent, I'll do the washing and ironing for a week."

Recalling the disaster the last time he did it, I shuddered at the thought. "Not in my house you won't."

From the Snacky, I made my way out to the car, climbed behind the wheel and started the engine, and while I waited for it to warm up, I rang Eric.

"I'm not making much progress here. Would it be possible to meet so we can work out where to go next?"

"Not possible, I'm afraid, Christine," he replied. "I'm on my way to London."

That came as a surprise. "Not chasing another job, are you?"

It was not as if it was any of my business, but I didn't fancy a new broom coming into Radio Haxford and sweeping the old rubbish away, by which I meant me.

"No, no. Nothing like that. I managed to get a word with Henry Fairburn last night, and I'm seeing him and his wife at one o'clock. I'll be back tonight, but it'll be late, so can we catch up tomorrow?"

"No problem. I might even know a bit more by then."

Chapter Seven

I spent the remainder of Thursday mooching round the house, making a half-hearted effort to track down the Walmers (to no avail) and then headed for CutCost where I met Dennis coming straight from work, much to his further irritation, but I brooked no argument.

"We need to stock the freezer and since you eat most of the frozen dinners, you can help me get them home."

"Rotten pack mule. That's what I am."

"Well giddy-up, Neddy, and let's get on with the job."

He followed me round the supermarket, his mood never changing, as a result of which, mine didn't improve, and that called to mind Eric's comments on the changes in me.

Not that it had any bearing on Dennis and me. We were just in a semi-permanent mood. I'd noticed it since the New Year, and I put it down to the short days and cold, dark nights, even though they were lengthening. We'd been together for thirty years and we'd had periods like this before; times when we didn't seem to get on well and they mostly coincided with the slow emergence from winter. Whatever was wrong, it would soon put itself right.

Things would get worse before getting better, however, and it started with a call from Eric while I was watching Dennis's all-day breakfast turning in the microwave. Don't ask why he wanted an all-day breakfast when he'd had one at Sandra's Snacky that morning. A full English was one of his favourite meals and he'd eat three or four a day if I let him.

"Good news," Eric told me. "I may have come across something which might help confirm your suspicions. A photograph of the Fairburns' stolen photograph frame."

There was a 'ding' but it wasn't an idea striking a light bulb in my head. It was the microwave oven telling me it was time to put the bacon and sausage back in with the baked beans, hash brown and omelette. Dennis liked the breakfast but he wasn't keen on the omelette and normally I would fry an egg to go with it, but I warned him that we were so late back from CutCost that it wouldn't happen. If nothing else, it would give him something else to moan about.

Eric was still talking. "I don't want to go into it over the phone. Could you meet me at Terry's tomorrow, say half past twelve. After I'm done with Reggie's morning stint?"

"No problem, but—"

"And on Saturday, you and I are going to Wealstun prison, near Wetherby, to see Prater."

"Oh. Are we? The thing is, you'd need a visiting order from—"

Eric cut me off for the second time. "Already arranged, and believe it or not I did it all over the phone. Once I told them who I was and what I wanted, without going into detail, naturally, both he and the prison authorities were happy for us to see him. He'll want to plead his case over the radio and the prison will expect a glowing mention in the broadcast.

I thought it must be nice to have such influence. "Right. Well in that case——"

A third interruption. I really would have to bring him to order. "Beryl's in the middle of serving dinner, so I'll get off and see you tomorrow."

And with that, he rang off. A second later, the microwave dinged for the second time to let me know Dennis's meal was ready.

I shouted him, and put the meal on the table, then, while he got stuck in, grumbling on the lack of fried egg, I accessed Google Maps on my smartphone and checked the distance to HMP Wealstun.

It was on the outskirts of Thorp Arch, a small village near Wetherby, where a huge trading/industrial estate had once stood. Still stood, for all I knew. I soon learned that Wealstun was an amalgamation of two prisons, and formed a sort of hybrid, of Category C and Category D. Cat C was those who could not be trusted, but were unlikely to escape, and Cat D was open, those who could be trusted not to escape, or holiday camps as Dennis preferred to call them.

I found this curious. Not Dennis describing open prisons as holiday camps, but Prater housed in a Cat C/Cat D prison. According to my research he was in Wakefield, which was Category A; i.e.

reserved for the most dangerous individuals, and it housed some of the most violent men in the UK, hence its nickname of 'Monster Mansion'. So how had he engineered a transfer to Cat C? I automatically assumed he was C and not D on the basis of his continued insistence of his innocence. Given Cat D, he might very well decide to hoof it back to Haxford in an attempt to prove that innocence.

Perhaps he had reconciled himself to his fate and settled down. He had, after all, spent twenty years in prison.

Dennis grunted and grumbled his way through his meal, and I settled for a cheese sandwich and a cup of tea while I mulled the things I had learned over the last day or two. I suppose my doubts stemmed from watching the video of Derek Tyndall's interview with the Scotland Yard detectives. For the life of me, however, I couldn't see what light a photograph of a photograph frame might throw on the matter, and when I put the point to Dennis, he was definite in his disinterest.

"Who cares?"

"I do, Dennis. It's my current case... sort of."

He pushed his empty plate to one side. "Let me tell you summat. If I had my way, Prater wouldn't have served twenty years in the slammer. He'd have served an hour on the end of a rope, cos that's how long they leave 'em swinging to make sure they're dead."

That brought out more irritation in me, mostly because it wasn't true. Not the bit about leaving them hanging for an hour. For all I knew that might have been correct. It was Dennis's attitude. Completely out of character. He believed in law and order, and he often considered our justice system to be too soft, but he was firmly anti-capital punishment on the grounds that they sometimes got it wrong and when that happened, there was no way to put it right.

I buried the anger. "Dennis, what's wrong?"

"Nowt."

"Yes, there is. You've been in a mood for days, maybe weeks, now."

"And you haven't?"

"Well, I was only chucking it back at you."

"And I say you started it. There's more important stuff than Radio rotten Haxford, you know."

This presented an even bigger puzzle, until I homed in on his meaning. "You mean sex. Have your forgotten Gaven Hall? And at our time of life—"

"I'm not talking about bedroom exercise."

Wrong again, and at that point, I lost it. "Then what are you talking about?"

"You're the one who's allus poking about on the Web. Do you know what's going on in the world? Have you heard about the cost of living crisis? The price of gas?"

I snapped back. "The price of ancient Morris Minors?"

He got to his feet. "No piddling point talking to you, is there?" And with that, he marched from the kitchen.

"That's because you're talking twaddle," I

shouted after him.

***

I didn't see Dennis on Friday morning. He was away to work before I got out of bed, and when I tried ringing him, all I got was his voicemail. Those of a generous disposition might say that he was too busy to answer the phone, but when I tried a second time and got his voicemail again, I knew he was sulking, and considering he had not been specific the previous evening, I still didn't know what he was talking about so I couldn't make any effort to put matters right.

But I knew a way of putting him in a more amenable frame of mind; a meat and potato pie.

Almost as I thought of it, I abandoned the idea. The last time I did it was to put right an argument between us during the McCrudden blackmail affair, and he never showed up because he was beaten up by those thugs involved on the periphery of the case. It seemed to me that if I went down that route, I might be tempting fate, and Dennis might not be so lucky next time.

Eventually, I decided on his second favourite meal: sausages and mashed potato, but it would have to be the right sausages. Not the frozen variety, but the pork and beef sausages sold by Silver's, my favourite butcher's stall in Haxford Market Hall. Where Dennis was concerned, such a meal might not have the same soothing effect as a meat and tater, but it would help. My grandma always told me that face powder might attract a man, but it took baking powder to keep him.

Thus decided, I rang Dennis again, but typically got his voicemail for the third time. I shut the call down, then rang Tony Wharrier who answered almost immediately.

"Hello, Christine. Unusual you ringing me. Is it about Jack Prater again?"

"No, Tony, it's about Dennis Capper."

"Well, he's next door, working on the monthly books, I think."

"I know where he is, but he's not speaking to me. Could you do me a favour? Pop next door and tell him to ring me on pain of death, and I mean within the next five minutes."

Tony chuckled. "I'll pass the message on."

Sure enough, three minutes later, Dennis rang and I made the connection. "What do you want, woman? I'm busy."

I ensured my tones were as curt as his. "So am I, Dennis. I have an appointment in town just after twelve o'clock."

"Eric Reitman trying to get you into bed again?"

"If that's how you choose to see it. While I'm in town, after Eric and I are through with our tryst, I'll buy sausages from Silver's. Don't be late home tonight. It's sausage and mash for tea."

The change in his attitude was instant. "Soss and mash? Don't worry…"

I didn't give him the chance to crawl into my good books. I cut the call there and then, and when he rang back a few minutes later, I ignored the call.

I was in Haxford Market Hall and settling into a

corner table at Terry's for 12:15, waiting for Eric. Despite the fracas between Dennis and me, there was work to be done, puzzles to solve. I hadn't done my shopping, having decided that it was not good form to turn up for a potential business meeting (we always held our meetings at Terry's) while carrying a pound of best beef bangers and a bag of Maris Piper spuds.

I'd just about finished my toasted teacake when Eric arrived carrying his bulky briefcase. He ordered tea for himself, and a fresh cup for me, and the usual round of small talk followed. How was I, how was Dennis, did I want to know how he and Beryl and his daughter Olivia were? I didn't really, but I did justice to the preliminaries before pressing him. It was necessary. Eric could be notoriously elliptical when he chose, and I preferred to get to the point.

"Can you tell me how a photograph is supposed to take us any further forward? I mean, with the best will in the world, I can buy photo frames as cheap as a fiver here in the market."

Sipping delicately at his tea, he placed his briefcase on an empty chair alongside our table, flipped up the lid, and took out a single photograph from a batch of about half a dozen. He placed it on the table, and turned it to face me.

Right away, I realised I wouldn't get this for a fiver. Large enough to accommodate an 8" x 6" photograph, I guessed it was sterling silver. It sported ears at all four corners, and an intricate, filigree design throughout.

"You don't know the Fairburns, do you?"

"Never heard of them until the other day," I

assured him.

"As luck would have it, I knew Henry, which was why he agreed to see me yesterday—"

"I remember you saying," I interrupted.

"Yes, well, Henry wasn't the key. It was his wife, Fiona. Terrible snob. Talks as if she's a member of the royal family, and she can't understand why she hasn't had an invite to the coronation, and I know for a fact she comes from somewhere quite ordinary. Somewhere like Chelmsford. Anyway, Henry had all but forgotten the break-in. He would, wouldn't he? Busy man, irons in too any fires. But Fiona knew. She's his second wife, and they were away on honeymoon at the time. The Seychelles."

I had to wonder whether Eric threw in that little gem just to emphasise the kind of people he routinely dealt with. "The Seychelles? Not Skegness?"

He laughed and went on with his explanation. "A houseproud woman, Fiona, and she had photographs of the house and contents as they were before the burglary. The photograph frame was in the centre of a shot of the grand fireplace. She let me take a picture of her photograph, and I've had our IT guys working on it this morning while I was directing Reggie's show. This—" he aimed a finger at the photograph "— is the result."

I opened my mouth to say something, but Eric got there first.

"Obviously, the photograph Fiona had contained an image of her and Henry on their wedding day, which they found torn up on the carpet after the burglary. It was still in the image Fiona had and our IT people had to cut it out while they were expanding the size of the image." He tapped the photograph. "All due respect, Christine, you won't buy a frame like that for five pounds. Sterling silver, filigree design, Fiona says – and she's never usually wrong about these things – it cost over £200."

I gave him a mock round of applause. "Great stuff, Eric. So now we know a whole lot of history about one item that was stolen in the burglary. I don't see what use it is to us."

He didn't answer right away, but took another wet of tea, and dipped into his briefcase again, bringing out another half-dozen large photographs. He cleared an area on the table and laid them down, all of them facing me.

Each image was of a decorative, silver frame, but each was different to the others, and all were different to the original. Those differences were tiny, almost unnoticeable in some cases, but they were there, and I began to have an inkling of what he intended.

"I rang the prison governor from London," he went on, "told him who I am, what it is I do, and what I was looking for, i.e. an interview with Jack Prater. He needed Prater's agreement, and he rang me back an hour later saying it was all fixed up for eleven o'clock tomorrow morning. With the best will in the world, Christine, I can't go into this alone. You're the ex-police officer, you're the professional private investigator, I need you there with me. Of course, if it's difficult…" He trailed off rather than stating the obvious.

"Aside from Dennis believing that you are one of my lovers, it's not difficult. According to my calculations, Wealstun is about forty miles. I can do it in, say, an hour."

He laughed again. "Lovers? You and me?"

"Don't worry about it. Dennis can't help being an idiot, can he?"

"Never mind Dennis. I know how Beryl would react." He chuckled again. "Anyway, you can save your petrol. What say I pick you up tomorrow morning at nine o'clock? There's a service area outside Leeds, Skelton Lake, and that's about twenty-five miles. We could stop there for coffee, finalise our approach. And you can reassure Dennis that I won't be booking us into the motel there." He narrowed an intense gaze upon me and gestured at the photographs. "You can see what I'm getting at, can't you?"

"You present Prater with this set of photographs, and ask him to tell you which one he stole from Fairburn House."

"Spot-on."

"And if he can't, we know, what?" This time, I didn't give him the opportunity to say anything. "He's been inside for the last twenty years, Eric. We don't know what that might have done to his memory, so from that point of view, it'll prove nothing."

"And suppose he can pick it out?"

"Again, it won't amount to definitive proof. He could guess, and he has a one in seven chance of getting it right. It could amount to pure luck."

"Not if he picks it out quickly enough. Even so, it gives us something to fight with, something we can take to the police. Am I right?"

I had to back down. "Fair enough. I can't think of any other way forward. Mandy Hiscoe won't be too ready to take us into her confidence, and if she's spoken to Paddy Quinn, he could be on the warpath."

He smiled. "Let's cross that bridge when we come to it."

Chapter Eight

Dennis was in a much improved mood after his meal, a traditional repast of the working man, but matters went downhill very quickly when I told him I would be out on Saturday morning.

"It's work, Dennis."

"You always grumble at me for working on a Saturday."

"It doesn't stop you, though, does it? I started this business, Dennis, and I have to see it through. If it's any consolation, it's not likely to be a pleasure trip. I'll be spending the morning in prison."

A cautious frown crossed his features. "Isn't that a bit risky?"

"Not really. I'll be with Eric Reitman."

And that announcement lit the blue touch paper. It was on a slow fuse, but with hindsight, it was obvious where it was going.

"Reitman? Again?"

"What's wrong with Eric?"

"Considering I don't know him that well, I don't know that there's anything wrong with him, but I do know he just about owns you. Didn't I say yesterday he's after bedding you?"

With tempers beginning to shred, I made the next accusation. "This is about that fried egg, on

Thursday night, isn't it?"

"No, it isn't. I don't give a hoot about a fried, flaming egg. If I wanted a fried, fizzing egg, I'd have done it myself."

"Don't make me laugh. You can't cook chips in the microwave without setting fire to the kitchen. So what is it then? The Morris Minor Greg Vetch sneaked from under your nose?"

"I don't give a toss about the Moggie."

(Note: as well as a soubriquet for domestic cats, Moggie (uppercase M) is also a nickname for the Morris Minor.)

"I'm on about Reitman," Dennis ranted. "He's got you in the palm of his hand and I'm worried about what other of your bits he might have in his hand."

I jabbed an angry finger into the table top. "For your information, he got me my contract with Radio Haxford."

"And what did Eric get in return?"

It was a familiar line. Like any other married couple, arguments reared their heads now and again, and for some reason known only to himself, Dennis always seemed to suspect infidelity. I don't know why. I'd never given any reason to think it, and I never would, unless he still had memories of the misleading conversation he overheard between me and Nathan Kalinsky. That was after Nathan tried and failed to get to my smalls. Dennis only heard a part of that exchange and it was ambiguous. It might have sounded like I was castigating Nathan after the event, but in fact I was railing him for even trying.

There again, Dennis worked with and around

enough people, Greg and Lester to name but two, who had broken marriages behind them. Even so, as far as I understood it, Greg's marriage fell apart because of his obsession with work – similar to Dennis's – and both of Lester's marriages foundered on his obsession with drink. I didn't drink, I didn't overwork, so whenever we got into the spats, Dennis opted for the third choice of marital disharmony: adultery.

I rounded on him again. "I'll tell you what Eric didn't get, and he never will. My knickers in his hand. All right? I will be at Wealstun prison tomorrow morning with him, working on our current case. And that's an end of it."

"And I'll be at work all day, so don't be surprised if the house is quiet when you get home."

For the second night in succession, no words passed between us, and on Saturday morning, on the dot of nine o'clock, Eric's BMW saloon (part of his remuneration package with Radio Haxford) arrived outside the front door.

I'd been up since half past seven, shortly after Dennis left for work. Cappy the Cat had been fed, watered, and granted permission to terrorise the birds in the back garden for a brief while, and as I joined Eric, he was safely locked in, sitting in the window, scowling at us, as if asking, 'where do you think you're going? I'm here, and I should have your exclusive attention'.

The day was warmish but overcast and I shivered as I climbed into the passenger seat. Not for long. The Beamer's heating system soon warmed me up while we struggled to get through

Haxford, and picked up the road for Huddersfield and Leeds.

A little less than forty minutes later, we stopped at Skelton Lake services, enjoyed a cup of coffee and a snack, and then climbed back into the car for the final twenty minute drive to Thorpe Arch and the prison.

During the early part of the journey conversation was minimal as Eric listened to radio Haxford and tutted and clucked at occasional glitches. Over coffee and croissants we talked the forthcoming coronation, and soon moved on to holidays. He and Beryl would be sunning themselves in Cape Verde come the late summer, Dennis and I had already talked about Lanzarote but taken no action. The way things were between us these last few days, I wasn't sure a week or a fortnight in Lanzarote was worth the expense or the effort.

Twenty minutes after leaving the service station, we pulled into the public parking area outside HMP Wealstun, and for the first time in a long time I thought Dennis may have a point when he described such places as holiday camps. There were no high, unscalable (is there such a word) concrete walls, only high fences, and the reception area bordered on the friendly.

Our bags were searched and anything which might conceivably be used as a weapon, including Eric's fancy, expensive fountain pen, was withheld, but they did allow us to take in a pocket recorder and the photographs, although they had to be transferred from Eric's briefcase into a plain, manila envelope.

From there we were escorted through to what was clearly an interview room. I was no expert on prisons, but I knew that the visiting area was always in the canteen, and I wouldn't fancy a meal in a cramped environment like the little room we were shown to.

Jack Prater was already waiting for us, a warder stood behind him, and in contrast to his friend, Derek Tyndall, the years had not been kind to Prater. His years of incarceration had taken their toll. Overweight, dumpy, whatever muscle he might have had on his arms, had long ago wasted to fat. His hair was almost gone, too, leaving a bald pate shining under the strip lighting, and his eyes reflected the emptiness of one who knew he would never taste freedom again.

After setting his pocket recorder on the table, Eric introduced us, tossed a pack of cigarettes and a disposable lighter alongside it and invited Prater to help himself, which he did. Neither Eric nor I smoked, but he guessed (rightly) that Prater did and would appreciate the gesture.

At a prompt from my director, I fired the opening salvo. "I'm an ex-police officer turned private eye. I worked the beat in Haxford during some of your glory days, and I was talking to an old pal of yours a couple of days ago; Derek Tyndall."

Not strictly true, but good enough for our man. He blew smoke at the ceiling and said, "Never heard of him."

I was prepared for the denial. "Curious. He speaks very highly of you. Reckons you're one of the best, especially when it comes to break-ins." Prater might have objected again, but I pressed on. "I didn't tell you where I saw him did I? He's on remand in Belmarsh, looking at a couple of years for burglary and various other offences." All right, so it was another lie. I didn't know where the video interview took place, but the tale would serve its purpose.

Prater pursed his lips in a noncommittal demonstration of only passing interest.

"He was particularly pleased with the job you and he did at Fairburn House."

"Never heard of it."

"Now, there you really do surprise me. You see, Prater, according to Tyndall, you and he were going through Fairburn House at about the same time as you were strangling Becky Walmer."

His hand shook visibly, and his frail features paled. A long silence followed, and both Eric and I guessed that the prisoner was trying to work out his response. It was a time for waiting, not a time for prompting, not a time for pushing.

When it came, it was a string of four-letter (and longer) words, a level of verbal abuse, which brought colour to my cheeks and ears, and put the accompanying warder on alert, but we maintained our silence.

"I told 'em," he said when he was calmer. "I told em at Haxford cop shop. I said I was somewhere else when she was snuffed."

Eric spoke up this time. "But you didn't tell them where you were or what you were doing, as a result of which you had nothing like a viable alibi, did you? According to the press, in your statement, you said you were full of drink and sleeping it off at your place, but no one other than Elaine Anguage could back that up and given her past, her word is worthless. You had no witnesses, and you couldn't name any of the pubs you'd been drinking in."

"That Kitson expected me to grass a mate up. The filth down south didn't have no one for that Fairburn job and I wasn't gonna give 'em Del. Not bloody likely. Haxford didn't have nothing on me for that girl and I knew I'd get off, so why would I sell a mate down the river? That's not how I work."

"You confessed," I pointed out.

"Up yours, missus. Kitson, he made me confess. I told 'em that in court. He knew who did that girl. So did I. So did everyone. But they wrapped it round me, didn't they, and we all went home happy... Everyone but me."

The interview was going largely as we expected, but Eric maintained our rearguard. "You know what, Prater, I don't think we believe you. We think this is Tyndall, bang to rights, trying to get an old pal off the hook."

"Well, you know what you can do, don't you?"

"And I'll tell you what I don't understand," I chipped in. "How come you and Tyndall are mates? You're a Yorkie. Haxford born and bred like me. You were at school with my old man and a couple of his mates. Tyndall was from South London."

Prater shrugged. "I've done my share of jobs in the big smoke. And we did time together in Birmingham, me and Del. We shared a cell, and we got out about the same time. About a year later, he rang me for the Fairburn blag. He needed someone who could shut down the alarms and I was the best. I don't know who tipped him off to the job, I don't know who was fencing the stuff, but the bottom line was sound. The couple were away. They had a security setup, sure. Silent bell at the local police station, but it was simple enough to silence at our end, and the cops down there were a waste of space and taxpayers' money. We knew we'd have a good twenty minutes, half an hour inside the place before they even got in their cars. That was enough time for us to clear out that big front room, and empty the safe." Prater laughed, much as Tyndall had on the illicit video. "Safe? I've seen tougher cash boxes hidden under the bed. We were back in the cars and making for the motorway before the first of the blue lights showed. Easy money, and it paid well. Apart from the five hundred and odd notes Del shoved me as my share of the moolah from the safe, I'd have at least another one and a half, two ton from selling off the tom and the other bits… if Kitson hadn't pinned Becky Walmer on me."

Eric frowned. "Tom?"

"Tom foolery," I translated. "Jewellery." (I know I mentioned it earlier, but my understanding didn't come from my days as a police officer. I got it from an old episode of *Poirot* I'd seen on TV.) I focussed on Prater. "You're not persuading me."

"Suit yourself, missus."

Eric opened the prison-supplied envelope and took out the stack of photographs. Opening the stopwatch facility on his smartphone, he laid the pictures on the table, turning each one to face Prater.

"I called to see the Fairburns yesterday, and they told me about one particular item which went missing. A photograph frame." He gestured at the photographs. "Which one is it, Prater? Show us." As he posed the question, he started the stopwatch.

The acid test. We both expected the prisoner to take his time studying the images. We were wrong. Almost the moment Eric put them down, Prater scanned the images and pointed at the image of Fiona Fairburn's photograph frame, the central image blurred to a smooth, dark brown, but the intricate filigree of the surround clear. "That's it. That's the one. Worth a bob or two if you had to go and buy it, and Del reckoned we'd get a couple of score for it."

Eric stopped his timer, made a point of collecting the photographs and storing them in the envelope, while I asked, "Why would Kitson pin it on you?"

Prater wagged a finger. "Try asking Kitson. I ain't saying nothing."

"Pity. You almost had us believing you then." Eric reached for the recorder, cigarettes and lighter. "I think we're through, don't you, Chrissy?"

Prater stayed us. "Hold on, hold on."

Eric hesitated and sat down again. Prater helped himself to a second cigarette, lit it, and this time blew the smoke directly at Eric.

"What's your game? Governor told me you were coming here to talk to me, sure, but I thought you was trying to spring me on a technicality or something."

With the first inkling that everything was going

in our direction, Eric said, "We don't play games, Prater. Not with criminals like you. You confessed to Becky Walmer's murder twenty years ago. You've spent those years in one nick or another. Now, one of your old pals says you were innocent, but Christine, who's the real expert, doesn't believe it, and I've been in the news game long enough to know that Tyndall wouldn't have kept his mouth shut all that time. He would have opened it, if only to his pals, other scum like you and him. Tyndall fed Scotland Yard this same honour amongst thieves rubbish, and I won't have it. There isn't any. If you want to convince us, then come up with a lot more than you are."

Prater took his time about answering, and as before, I guessed that he was measuring his response. Crushing out his smoke, he helped himself to a third, made a show of lighting it, and when he did speak, it was in the same confrontational manner he had employed since the interview began, and it was aimed straight at me.

"You know what you and your pals never did? You never looked at that girl. You didn't look at your own, either, but then, what can you expect from the filth? Kitson set his sights on me and didn't look anywhere else. So why don't you try doing what he didn't do?"

This was a similar hint to those from Wynn Anguage and Nancy Farmer. "And what was it he didn't do?" I asked.

"I just told you. He didn't look at his own, and none of his own looked at her."

I shook my head. "You'll have to do better than

102

that, Jacko. Give me some names."

"No names. I don't do that kinda stuff. I didn't grass Del up, did I? And why? Cos I knew they didn't have nothing on me for that lass. Besides I told you what to do, didn't I? Look at the little tart and talk to Kitson."

"You obviously knew her."

"So did most of Haxford."

Definitely the same message the two women had given me.

Satisfied that the recording would remind him, Eric picked up his recorder and stopped it. He gestured at the cigarettes and lighter. "Yours, with our compliments. Speaking to Kitson could be difficult. He's retired."

"Yeah." Prater snorted again. "So I read. Sodded off to live in Spain or somewhere. What you do is up to you, but I'll tell you this. My lawyers'll get to know about what Del's said ten minutes after you leave, and I'll be outta here before the end of the month."

I gave a throwaway shrug. "It's not like I care one way or the other, but if you want to talk to me at any time, just make sure I know where to find you."

Truth was, I did care. Eric's cleverly designed test proved it to me. Just as I had warned, it did not constitute definitive proof of Prater's part in the burglary at Fairburn House, which would clear him of Becky Walmer's murder, but it would go a long way in court to declare his conviction unsafe.

Like me, Eric was satisfied. Back in his car, he showed me the stopwatch display which read 1.7 seconds. "Look at the time it took for him to pick

103

out that frame. A quick glance and he pointed straight to it. That man is innocent. He should have served a maximum five years for housebreaking, not twenty years for murder."

"I agree," I said, "but the courts might take a different view."

"You're the expert, Chrissy. Where do we go from here?"

It didn't take a lot of thinking about. "The police, I should think, but we'll have to tread carefully. Technically, legally, I don't think I was supposed to watch that video, and I certainly shouldn't have shown it to you."

He started the engine and pulled out of the car park. "And you think they'll threaten us with arrest or something?"

"I can sweet talk Mandy Hiscoe, but if Paddy Quinn's involved, anything is possible."

"In that case, you still haven't learned the power of radio."

I didn't know it for another hour and a half, but Paddy and Mandy were ahead of us and waiting outside the house when Eric pulled into Bracken Close.

And it was Mandy who read out the formal caution.

"Christine Capper, Eric Reitman, I'm arresting you both for possession of confidential material, the property of the Metropolitan Police. I must caution you, that you do not have to say anything…"

The rest of her words were lost to me.

Chapter Nine

Paddy glowered across the table at me. "The Met are quizzing one Detective Constable Ivan Jephcott. He was part of the team who arrested and interrogated Tyndall, and he was the one who sent the video to you. He's admitted it."

Faced with an angry Mandy and a furious Paddy, I shrugged. "Yes? And?"

While she was little cooler, Mandy was far from friendly. "You used to be one of us. You know the rules. You should have brought that video to us. I asked you on Tuesday where you got your information from and you wouldn't tell me."

"Because I didn't know where it came from. I dug out the email for you and let you read it. It was anonymous. I recalled the text messages and let you see them when you arrested us, and my all record tells you he rang me, but nowhere at any time, did he give me a name, phone number, or genuine email address. He just insisted it was a miscarriage of justice and I should investigate."

"You should still have brought it to us."

"And let you bury it?" When I got no answer to my protest, I pressed on. "Besides, how was I supposed to know he was a cop?"

At this point, Paddy chipped in. "Who else

would send it?"

During the forty minutes since our arrest and incarceration in separate holding cells while the police prepared the interview room, I'd had plenty of time to consider the problem, anticipate their questions, and I had a ready answer. "Prater's solicitor?"

"Bull," Paddy snapped. "We've already spoken to her. This morning while you were sucking up to Prater. She knows nothing about it."

"I meant Tyndall's solicitor. He's bound to be a Londoner so he wouldn't get involved in a case this far north, would he?"

"He wasn't there when the Yard interviewed Tyndall," Paddy pointed out.

Mandy came in full throttle. "And if he had been, he'd have sent it to Prater's lawyer."

"Or someone who might decide to demonstrate an attempted cover up by the filth." As my temper reached new heights, a point occurred to me, and I backed off a little. "Just a minute. How do you know I was visiting Prater this morning? You haven't asked me where I was, so did Eric tell you?"

"We haven't spoken to Reitman yet. We figured you were the easier target."

That comment almost had me reaching across the table for his throat. "Have you forgotten who you're dealing with? I'm Christine Capper. Remember? Ex-cop and a radio star. I have influence…"

Oh, dear lord. What had I just said?

It was the cause for much amusement on the other side of the table and that served to fuel my temper further "Who told you?" I shouted. "Who told you we'd been to see Prater?"

Paddy gave me a confident yet sly smile. "Dennis, actually. When we couldn't find you at home, we went to his workshop and he said, quote, 'she's gone to some nick near Wetherby', unquote. It didn't take us long to put that together and a quick call to Wealstun told us the rest."

That did it. My temper reached an explosive peak and Dennis would know about it when I saw him. For all his pretence that he didn't listen, the reality was he never missed a word I said.

For now, I waved a wild hand at the room in general and I was shouting loud enough to be heard three streets away. "Go ahead and book me, if that's what you're gonna do, but it's in the public domain now, and if I don't get it out to the mainstream press, I guarantee Eric will. He knows people who will nail your arses to the wall."

Mandy recoiled in shock, and as it occurred to me what I'd just said, so did I.

Paddy calmed down right away, and when he spoke it was as if we were old friends. "In all the years I've known you, Christine, I've never heard you use language like that."

His use of my full name spelled out his shock, and he had a point. I'd never heard me use language like that either. Dear God. Eric was right. I was beginning to behave like a spoiled celebrity.

I backed off. "I... I'm sorry. You're right. It's not like me. But it does show how annoyed I am. You're harassing me for watching a video of an official police interview, when you should be out there finding out who really did kill Becky Walmer and who fitted Jack Prater up."

Whether it was down to my uncharacteristic outburst or an attitude of 'I'm sick of this verbal ping-pong', I don't know, but Paddy maintained his equilibrium. "No one is covering anything up, Chrissy. We never did. When we got the original message from the Met, we looked at the case and there was no fresh evidence. As I understand, Mandy has already told you that we can't take the word of a man like Tyndall, and we all know Jack Prater. He can lie for Great Britain, especially when he's trying to save his own skin. He was at the Walmer's place that night. We know that. He confessed and the fact that he waited until he was in court before retracting his confession makes it doubly certain that he killed her."

This was a revelation to me. "He was definitely there?"

"Incontrovertible evidence," Mandy was as calm as her boss. "He left traces. Enough for CID to pin him down, and as Paddy said, once he was confronted with that, he confessed. Since then, no other evidence has come to light. As far as we're concerned, the conviction is safe."

I began to see some light in the way ahead. "Sorry, Mandy, but you mean *you* have no evidence." I stressed the word 'you'. "Eric and I have."

My announcement took them both aback. "What?" she asked.

I ran through the brief experiment Eric had carried out with Prater. "When it came to the

108

crunch, Jacko took less than two seconds to identify the frame stolen from the Fairburns."

Paddy fell back on legalese. "A lucky shot. That's all."

"The courts might not think so, especially when Prater gives them a detailed list of the things he and Tyndall stole. And the last thing Prater told us this morning was he'd be talking to his lawyer. You said she didn't know anything. Well she will by the time Prater's through, and she'll kick up a bigger stink than Radio Haxford. And if he really is innocent, you can expect a visit from the IOPC asking why you've been sitting on it."

This time it was Paddy who resorted to cursing, and his choice of language was a good deal stronger than anything I had said. When he calmed down (at Mandy's insistence) he switched tactics. "You're calling into question the reputation of a distinguished detective."

"Kitson? You mean a boor and a sexist bully?"

Now the inspector sneered. "I wondered when we'd get round to the gender argument." He pushed on before I could pick the argument up. "Pete Kitson's personal life has no bearing on his professionalism."

"He obviously never tried to get you into bed," I snarled, and I noticed Mandy's lip curl into the vaguest hint of a smile before she wiped it clean.

And it was Mandy who took up the debate. "All this is getting us nowhere. The fact is, Chrissy, you were in possession of official police evidence and you had no right to view it. Worse, you shared it with Eric Reitman, but you didn't share it with us.

As far as we're concerned, that's an offence. Withholding potential evidence possibly pertinent to a crime. And I did insist on Tuesday that if you heard anything, anything at all, you should bring it to us."

My confidence began to return and I remained defiant. "Then book me and let me get off home."

Paddy shrugged. "Very well. Christine Capper, you will be reported for withholding information possibly prejudicial to a police investigation..."

***

It was getting on for three when I came out of the police station. They had Eric to interview, so I didn't wait. Instead, I got a taxi to Haxford Mill. I didn't have much choice. They'd brought me to the station in a patrol car, and I wasn't going home to collect my car before giving my other half the benefit or otherwise of my fury.

I found him buried in a sea of paperwork. There was no sign of Lester – the public bar of the Engine House (known locally as the Sump Hole) would be a good bet – but Greg was in the pit, working under a car and I could hear Tony pottering about in the body shop next door. By body shop, I mean the area where they dealt with bodywork, not a shop full of ethically produced cosmetics. I'm not quite sure what Tony Wharrier would do with skin care and other lotions and potions, and good as they were, I couldn't see them being much use on the rust encrusted body of an old Ford Fiesta.

As I'm often at pains to point out, Dennis had

always been the kind of man who would say what was on his mind and worry about the consequences afterwards. It was easy for him. A shade under six feet tall, a non-smoker, light drinker, his job kept him fit and strong and he didn't worry much about others. Even when those thugs attacked him, he fought back. I was a tiny, five feet four inches, and much more diplomatic than him, but even so there were times (like now) when I didn't care who heard me.

"When will you learn to shut your sodding trap?"

Amazed? He couldn't have been more stunned if I'd stripped off before him and said, 'come on then, give me your best shot'.

"What are you talking about, woman?"

"The two hours I've just spent at the police station after you opened your gob and told them where I was this morning, that's what." I was so incensed, I didn't register that Greg's spanners had stopped tippy-tapping.

"I didn't know it was top secret did I?"

"Where I am, what I'm doing is no business of anyone but mine. Especially not the police."

"Considering we're wed, I reckon it's my business too."

"I'll call it a day, Cappy." It was Greg's voice from behind me. I turned to find him stood there, looking awkward and embarrassed.

"Bit early, Herriot," Dennis said, completely ignoring me.

"Yeah, but by rights, you and Chrissy should take your fight outside or home. I don't wanna listen in, so I'll go. I'll catch you Monday." He moved to his locker, pulled on his coat, fished out his car keys, and with a curt nod, walked out.

Dennis glowered at me. "Now look what you've done."

"I don't care. You have no business telling Paddy Quinn where I was."

"What's this Paddy Quinn stuff? It were our Simon as rang me. And he never said nowt about it being police business. He said he'd been to our place and couldn't find you. End of. So I told him where you were."

If that wasn't enough to take the wind out of my sails, Tony Wharrier, putting in an appearance from next door, helped.

"Good afternoon, Christine. I heard what Greg said, and although it's none of my business, he does have a point you know. I mean, Val and I fall out often enough, but we keep our arguments between us. Frankly, you two could probably be heard in the Snacky, three floors up."

For the second time that afternoon I found myself apologising. "Yes, I'm sorry, Tony. But I got back about lunchtime and suddenly found I was under arrest."

It wasn't only Tony who reacted, but Dennis too. "You were arrested? What for?"

"Just forget it, Dennis. Tell me what Simon told you."

"I've just told you. He said he'd been to ours, there was no one in. He tried to ring you and couldn't get through, so he rang me and asked what you were up to. So I told him. As far as I was

112

concerned, it was either him or Nam who wanted to speak to you. He never said nowt about Paddy Quinn sending him."

The focus of my anger spun like a weathervane in a gale, but couldn't find a home. First Dennis, now Simon, now Mandy, now Paddy. And DI Quinn was the prime target. He lied to me. He insisted that they had come to the mill to speak to Dennis. He would know the next time I saw them. And so would Mandy. She knew he was lying.

For the time being, I vented my frustration on Dennis. "Her name is Naomi, not Nam."

"She likes Nam."

"Anyway, you can get off your behind and take me home."

"I'm in the middle of a days' work."

"No. You're at the end of a day's work, and I am not forking out for a second taxi."

It was Tony who persuaded him. "You go, Dennis. I'll lock up when I'm finished."

With much chuntering and slamming about, he took off his overalls, dug out his coat and led the way to his pride and joy, a 1979 Morris Marina. Minutes later, we were on our sedate way home. If it had been my car or the works van, Dennis would have been rushing, but he never rushed his precious Marina.

"If you treated me with half the respect you treat this piece of junk, maybe we'd get on a bit better."

"And if you paid me half the attention you do those clowns at the radio station, we might get on better."

113

"That's not fair. They don't own me."

"Well, you could have fooled me. Reitman's only got to snap his fingers and you're sweeping up after him. And look what he's got you involved in now. Trying to get a lag like Prater out of the nick, and you've been arrested for it. What did you do? Try to smuggle him out disguised as a human bean?"

The fury was building up again and it's a good job Dennis was driving. If we'd been stationary, I'd have hit him with my handbag.

"For your information, it was me who dragged Eric into this business and not the other way round, and no, we didn't try to bring Prater out, but we did get evidence that might help prove him innocent."

"Well, excuse me if I don't throw a party for him."

We were pulling into the drive when Eric rang, much to Dennis's further disdain. "Mr wonderful again? Ask him if he knows how far he's dropped you in it."

"Shut up, Dennis. Yes, Eric?"

"Sorry, Christine. Is this a bad time? Only you don't sound too happy with Dennis."

"Forget it, Eric. I told you, he thinks you're one of my lovers."

"Only one of them?" He chuckled and then became serious. "The police are reporting me for watching that video."

"Same here," I replied. "Don't worry. It'll all come right when we find the real killer."

He was silent for a moment. "Did you hear what I said, Christine? I've been reported. They actually came looking for me at Radio Haxford this morning, and as the police released me, I got a call from the studio. The big boss wants to see me on Monday. I'll probably get a formal warning and when he's through with me, he'll probably want to see you."

The fire began to rise in me again. "I don't work for him, Eric. I work for me, and if he wants to tear up my contract, let him carry on. As long as he pays me. But remember this, and if you won't tell him, I will. I'm a professional and respected private investigator, and I'm on the trail of something rotten here. I will not let it go."

Chapter Ten

The events of Saturday would have far-reaching consequences. The mood between Dennis and me did not deteriorate but it didn't improve either. He even went to work on Sunday morning, something he hadn't done for many a year, and I guessed it was a case of anything to avoid me. Worse than that, I didn't mind. Anything to avoid him.

I spent most of Sunday mooching around the house, making some kind of effort to track down the Walmer family, without success. It made a kind of sense. I remembered the publicity after Becky's murder, and I guessed that as a family, they wanted their privacy, and even now they keep the whole nasty business behind them.

Monday was a public holiday in England and we would normally float off down to the Wool Fair or even the seaside, but Dennis chose to work again and I ended up spending the afternoon with Naomi and my darling granddaughter, Bethany at that same Wool Fair, and then in mufti again until Dennis got home about six o'clock. Even then, he still did not want anything to do with me and responses to my routine queries were greeted with taciturn grunts.

Things began to hot up on Tuesday morning. As always, my agony aunt spot and debrief were over and done with by half past eleven, but I couldn't just leave the studio. When I first arrived, at half past ten, Eric brought me up to speed on events so far.

"It's bad. I was called in front the big boss yesterday – a bank holiday, if you please – given a formal warning, and ordered to drop the investigation into Jack Prater's conviction."

"And you accepted it? Just like that?" I snapped my fingers to emphasise the point.

"I'm employed by the station, Chrissy. I'm not on a contract like you, Reggie and the other presenters. The big boss really is my boss. The police came here on Saturday morning looking for me, and from the boss's point of view, that could bring the station into disrepute." He hesitated a moment. "He wants to see you after your agony aunt slot. I'm warning you in advance, he's not in a very good mood, and he will read you the riot act. If you try to ignore him, he'll tear up your contract for everything; agony aunt, mystery hour, and Lost Friends."

The anger which had driven me for most of the previous week and which had increased over the weekend, bubbled to the surface once more. "He can do as he pleases. I told you once before, as long as he pays me what I'm owed, I'm fine with that." Another point occurred to me. "Tell me something. Why is everyone so afraid of using his name? I mean, for God's sake, I've been with you for nine months now, and I still don't know who he is."

"He's a money man, Christine. Radio Haxford is only one of the pies he has fingers in, but he is the majority shareholder and he's the officially appointed controller. As far as Radio Haxford is concerned, his word is law, and frankly, I have too much to lose to ignore him."

I was so angry that during my slot, I fluffed my lines a couple of times causing DJ, Reggie Monk to pass a few ribald comments after I signed off. Eric commented on them too, before pointing me upstairs to the rarefied domain of the big boss.

I didn't even know there was an upstairs to the studio. Well, I suppose I did, but it had never impinged on my consciousness. It consisted of nothing more than a small, outer office, with a frosted glass door behind the PA's station, which led to a slightly larger office.

Panoramic windows, similar to those of an airport control tower surrounded us, giving us a grand, 360° view of Haxford town centre, or should I say the roof of the market hall, and the upper levels of several tall buildings in the immediate vicinity, beyond which was nothing but a perturbed sky through which an occasional spot of sunshine tried to show.

According to the little plaque on the forward edge of his desk, the big boss was none other than James Langdon. Langdon, Longjohn, I nearly had it right. I also had the feeling that I'd heard of him, but if that were so, it must have only been in passing. In reality, I wouldn't know him if I ran over him on the High Street, and Haxford High Street is a pedestrian zone. (Question to self and those of you paying attention: have I already used that simile?)

I guessed him to be about sixty years of age.

Tall, a head of thinning, dark hair, with an angry gleam in his ice blue eyes, he appeared as a broad shouldered, physically fit and athletic man. Dressed in a dark suit, white shirt and midnight blue tie, his hands were clasped on the desk ahead of him, but I noticed that the skin was smooth, unruffled, untainted by any trace of physical work in his history.

There was nothing on the desk other than the blotter, and a mobile telephone set off to one side, but his in and out trays were laden with documents. He did not offer to shake hands, but nodded towards the empty chair opposite him, and as I took the seat, he retrieved a single document from one of the trays and laid it on the desk in front of him.

"Your actions, Capper, are threatening to drag this station's reputation into the gutter." The voice was smooth, even, but it was impossible to mistake the determination. "I've been the controller here ever since we first went on air, and never, in all that time, have we been visited by the police seeking to take one of our employees in for questioning, and yet, on Saturday, CID were here in force looking for you and Eric Reitman. I later learned that you both were arrested, and reported for withholding information from the police. I will not have that. I'm ordering you now to cease all enquiries into the conviction and incarceration of Jack Prater."

Disregarding most of the flowery language, I resorted to traditional Capper candour. "And if I refuse?"

"People don't refuse me."

"You mean other people don't refuse you." I

stressed the words 'other people'.

He picked up the document. "This is your contract with Radio Haxford. None of your programmes are doing particularly well. You either drop the investigation or I tear up the contract now."

Determined, burning with anger, I stood my ground. "Go ahead. Tear it up. As long as you make sure you pay me what I'm owed… up to the end of the two-year contract."

He actually laughed. "Who do you think you're dealing with? You think I'm some graduate noddy, fresh out of university, who couldn't tell the difference between the end of a ballpoint pen and a cricket bat? There's a clause in this contract, which states that if you take any action which threatens the good name and reputation of the station, the contract will be declared null and void, and you will be paid only for the work you've already carried out."

Determined as ever to get under his skin, I pointed out, "Good name and reputation are the same thing. There's something you should know, Langdon—"

"That's Mr Langdon to you."

"And it's Mrs Capper, not Capper." I paused to let the lesson sink in. "I am an ex-police officer and a professional private investigator, licensed and registered with a regulatory authority, and it's part of my calling, part of that same regulatory authority's code of conduct that I be honest and truthful. Jack Prater has served twenty years for a crime he did not commit—"

"You don't know that."

"I do know it. I can't prove it yet, but I will

make it my business to do so. There's something else you should know, Mr Langdon. My brother is a respected solicitor, well versed in civil as well as criminal law. You are trying to silence me, threatening to withhold fees due to me under the terms of the contract, in order to shut me up, and if you persist, I will see you in court. The one thing I will not do is drop the investigation into Jack Prater's conviction." I pointed a shaking finger at the contract. "Now do as you will."

Without more ado, he tore the contract in half and then half again.

I came away from the studio and made my way to Terry's in a state of conflicting emotions. I had stood my ground against a man who preferred to live in the shadows, a man who was obviously a bully, not afraid to use his clout to get what he wanted. That was probably the reason he stayed in the background. On the other hand, I'd lost a valuable source of income and I would have a fight on my hands to collect what was owed to me.

It prompted memories of Gaven Hall. I had a fight on there, too. A dogmatic DCI from the Cambridgeshire force, an aggressive young man (the best man at the wedding as it happened) who tried to meet me head on, an elderly academic who played on his age and apparent frailty, and of course, Sir Kingsbury Gaven, part of the nation's landed gentry, a peer of the realm.

It was the same at Allbrook Farm. Both Alan Allbrook's and Lenny Keogh's attitude left a lot to be desired, but in neither case did I back away, and when I thought about it, it was the same during the

McCrudden affair, and the Leach case, in fact every difficult case I'd encountered. Wise men (and women) didn't argue with Christine Capper.

By the same token, I wasn't actually sure I'd come head to head with someone who enjoyed the same clout as James Langdon, not even Sir Kingsbury Gaven, and I realised I might just be on a loser.

I settled down in Terry's with a cup of tea and not one but two toasted teacakes. Comfort eating.

Where did that notion come from? Ask Lester Grimes and his idea of comfort food would be a pint of Haxford Best Bitter and two pork pies. I didn't like beer and I couldn't stand pork pies. The last time I ate one (so long ago, I couldn't remember when) I'm sure I put on at least half a stone. Besides, in a town like Haxford, pork pies were not a woman's food. They were the exclusive province of men, while women indulged in fondant fancies and toasted teacakes.

But *two* toasted teacakes at one sitting? That was not even comfort eating. It was sheer greed and it was motivated by self-pity. I was feeling sorry for myself, and in that respect, it could be diagnosed as comfort eating, or more accurately, comfort gluttony. I was trying to drown my sorrows in fruit teacakes, toasted to a golden brown and lathered in Lurpak (or whatever butter Terry used).

Everyone, so it seemed, was against me. Dennis had taken every opportunity to have a go at me for the last week or more, entertaining idiotic suspicions of me and other men, yet failing to get to the specifics of what was really wrong. My best friend

122

on the police force had arrested and charged me for what was (as far as I was concerned) a legal technicality, and Eric, the man who encouraged me into radio, had shown a singular lack of backbone. His status, his livelihood, his salary, and company supplied, upmarket wheels were more important to him than justice. He had chickened out and tried to get me to go along with him in order to pacify Langdon.

To my disappointment, I learned that I couldn't cope with two teacakes and half of the second one remained on the plate. Typical. It summed up my putative radio career. Couldn't finish what I started.

Even though I was inside the market hall, that last thought made me feel as if the sun had just emerged and bathed me in its beatific illumination. Maybe I couldn't bring an end to my short radio career covered in glory, but as a private eye, I never left anything unfinished.

The truth began to seep through. If nothing else, the events at Gaven Hall which almost persuaded me for the second time to give up my PI licence were offset by the outcome at Christmas Manor, which persuaded me not to relinquish it. Coupling that to my determination to prove Jack Prater's innocence told me that if I was not cut out for media stardom, I was nevertheless, what I was meant to be: Haxford's best, Haxford's *only* licenced private investigator.

Less than a year ago, Reggie Monk approached me at this very same café and asked me to take over the agony aunt slot from Lizzie Finister. Soon after, Eric asked me to go with Lost Friends, and before much longer, the mystery hour came into being. I went along with it, tempted by dreams of a jackpot-sized income and local, if not national fame. Everything else became secondary, until my meeting with Langdon pushing me to compromise my standards, and I wouldn't do it.

Why should I be downhearted? How many times did we whine and complain over celebs who behaved in this same manner; abandoned their standards, their beliefs in favour of pots of money and fame? And then, when they had everything, fell into the attitude of 'I'm me, I'm *the* most important, and up yours the rest of you'? And I wanted to be one of them? I was becoming one of them? Never. Never in a millennium plus one.

With this realisation, I also understood Eric's stance. He was part of that same setup, the modern ethos which Dennis despised so much, the attitude I was so scornful of. Perhaps Eric was not as bad as the more outrageous celebs, but I couldn't blame him for doing what he had to do in order to ensure his and his family's livelihood and comfort. By the same reasoning, I had no reason to flagellate myself for refusing to become part of it.

With that, I felt so much more at ease, and wolfed down the remaining half of teacake, before finishing my tea.

I was about to leave, when Eric and Reggie Monk joined me just after half past twelve. Reggie was his usual, cheerful self, right down to the body odour and halitosis (I do wish he'd see a dentist and make better use of deodorants. No wonder he was twice divorced). He went to the counter while Eric sat with me.

He was clearly downcast and obviously irritated. "You decided you'd rather call it a day?"

"After Langdon's efforts to paint me into an inescapable corner, yes. He tore up the contract, he's refusing to pay me, and I've told him, he'll hear from my solicitor."

"You're not entirely out of the game, Chrissy. I persuaded him that you're too popular as the agony aunt, so you'll still be with us every Tuesday."

"Thank you, Eric."

"It's a damn shame," Reggie said, placing three cups of tea on the table. "I said all along that you were a natural for radio, Chrissy."

"You did. You both did, and I don't want either of you to think I'm ungrateful for your help and encouragement, but if it means compromising my principles, then, I'm sorry, but I don't want it. As for anything I'm owed, I warned Langdon that he'll be hearing from my brother."

Reggie laughed. "What's he gonna do? Crack the big boss over the head with a bottle jack?"

Eric shook his head, and I tutted. "My brother, Stephen, is a lawyer, Reggie. My husband, Dennis, is the mechanic. You should know. Dennis services your car."

"Oops. Sorry."

Eric's comment was more to the point. "It won't do you any good, Christine. Langdon will simply claim your actions were in danger of bringing the station into disrepute. How many times do I have to repeat that we're a community entertainment channel, not news?"

I wouldn't have it. "Langdon tried to silence me. As far as I'm concerned, that's coercion. It makes you wonder what he's afraid of. He and the station could bask in the glory as and when I prove my case against the police. But not now. I'll go public on the entire issue if I have to."

Now Reggie tutted. "It won't alter anything, Chrissy. Terminating your contract is a civil matter, and as an ex copper, you should know that they rest on balance of probability, not beyond reasonable doubt. It'll be your word against his, and he can throw more money at it than you."

"He'll still take the flak," I pointed out as my smartphone warbled for attention. "Excuse me." I took the phone out of my bag, picked up an unknown number and hoping that it might be the mysterious Constable Jephcott, I made the connection and apologised to the two men again before announcing myself. "Christine Capper."

"Now then, you old bat," said a voice I had not heard in years." You rang the mall on Thursday, but I've only just come back to work after a long weekend off."

I laughed. "Linda Risley. How are you, you old hag?"

Eric and Reggie gaped at the repartee.

"All the better for hearing from an old buddy. What did you want?"

With one eye on my (former) radio colleagues, I replied, "It's too complicated to go into over the phone. Can we meet?"

"Sure. You know where Tenderwood Mall is?"

"I do."

"Can you get here for three? Bell me as you park up and I'll make sure I'm on a break. Give me a clue to what you want."

"Becky Walmer and Jack Prater."

"Oh. Right." Was I mistaken or was that a note of caution in her voice? She went on, "I'll catch you at three."

I ended the call and smiled at my (former) colleagues. "If you gentlemen will excuse me, I have business to attend to… the business of proving Jack Prater innocent."

Chapter Eleven

Tenderwood Mall sat on the outskirts of north Huddersfield, just off the A629, Halifax Road. It was a standard, out-of-town (if only by a mile or two) shopping centre fronted by one of the better quality supermarkets, and every conceivable shop known to High Street Woman could be found within its lower and upper gallery. At one time, there was also a cinema, but when I walked into the temperature controlled environment, I discovered that it had shut down. I guessed that people no longer had the money for cinemas. Dennis wouldn't entertain such places.

"Fifteen quid to watch a fillum? I remember when it was five bob." It was a lie. Dennis was still a toddler when Great Britain did away with pounds, shillings, and pence.

Linda Risley was a couple of years younger than me, just past her big 5-0, but the years had not been kind to her. She was what I would describe as 'chunky'. Others, less generous than me, would say 'fat', but her eyes still shone with pleasure, and there was a generous smile about her jowly features when we met and hugged outside Costa.

She joined the police about two years after me, and during her probationary year, we become good mates. As I left the service she opted for CID, and at the time of Becky Walmer's death, she was a DC working alongside the more experienced and soon to be Detective Sergeant, Paddy Quinn. Both were seconded to Kitson's team for the Walmer inquiry.

I recalled those early days with great fondness. A couple of drinks after the end of a shift, delight in fending off the blatant passes of other officers, and generally having a good time of it before going home to our respective partners.

I left the service when I discovered I was preggers with Simon, but she carried on for another ten years or so before she was beaten up in a brawl. I visited her in hospital and that's when she told me the tale, or as much of it as she could remember.

A fight had broken out in the Woolcombers, a popular pub in Haxford. Uniformed were short-handed so she and Paddy Quinn went in to help. Paddy got thumped on the nose, but for all his faults, he was a tough cookie and fought back. It was only after things had calmed down that they found Linda on the ground, spark out after someone had hit her with the proverbial blunt instrument (never actually itemised amongst the broken bits of furniture, fixtures, and fittings) and proceeded to give her a good kicking while she was down. There were several prosecutions from that brawl, but her attacker was never identified, and when she came to the end of her sick leave, she put in her notice.

"Best move I ever made, even if I do have to work through the coronation," she told me as we settled at a table with a coffee and couple of cakes. "And you don't seem to be doing badly out of semi-retirement, do you? Radio star now." She cackled. "I still live in Haxford, you know... well, north Haxford. And I'm a regular listener to your Lost Friends show."

"Not the agony aunt?"

"You don't have any answers for my problems, girl." She patted her large belly. "A means of getting this off for good, and getting horizontal more often, preferably with some hunk."

We both laughed, but her comment forced the question. "Are you not with Robin anymore?"

"Course I am, but he's getting too old for it." She abruptly changed the subject. "Hey, I heard about your Dennis last year. I felt for him. Same thing as happened to me at the Woolcombers."

I nodded. "Difference is we caught the scum that battered Dennis. Paddy and co never did get whoever hit you, did they?"

"I got over it. Did Dennis?"

"He's as sound as a pound these days. Grumpy as ever. And you know Paddy's moved on, don't you?"

She laughed again "An inspector no less. I suppose he takes after Pete Kitson."

"And talking of Kitson..." I trailed off to take a mouthful of coffee.

Linda's features darkened. "Yeah. You mentioned Prater and Becky. What's to do, girl?"

I had to steel myself to tell her. "I've uncovered evidence that Prater might just be innocent." I hastened on as her features twisted into a mask of disbelief. "Nothing concrete. Nothing definite, but enough to suggest that he was somewhere on the

130

outskirts of London at the time Becky was murdered."

She shook her head. "No way. It was him. Listen, Chrissy, I was there. I was on the team. So was Paddy. When we got there, Kitson and his pal, Penning, were in mufti, waiting for scientific support. They got us and a bunch of uniforms on the door to door, while they waited for forensics. Next thing we knew, they had threads taken from under Becky's fingernails. DNA was through in a matter of hours and it was Jacko's. He was there. He did it."

"I spoke to him, Linda. In prison. He still denies it. And as for the forensic evidence, you and I both know that there are ways and means of setting up a body for scientific support to find what you want them to find."

She backed off a little. "Well, yeah, but this is Kitson we're talking about. He was a scumbag, for sure, especially with the women. I should know."

That took me by surprise. "He sweet talked you into bed?"

"Only the once. He must have tried it with you."

"He did, but it got him exactly nowhere."

"Oh. Mind, you were never interested in CID, were you? Anyway, like I said, he was a piece of dog crap, but he was a straight piece of dog crap. No way would he falsify evidence." There was a pause. "Spoken to him, have you?"

"Not yet, he's retired. Lives in Spain now."

"That's what the police pension can do for you. What about his mate, Penning?"

"I have him to find."

"He's here in Huddersfield. Lives in the Longwood area, I think."

I made a mental note to track him down. "Listen, Linda, you were there. Was there never any other suspect?"

"Nope."

"Did you learn much about Becky?"

"Little angel according to mummy and daddy. According to everyone else she had the fastest freefall knickers in Haxford. A class one tramp."

That called to mind Wynn Anguage's opinion, and I also recalled that Prater had hinted at it during our prison meeting, and indeed, before Prater, Nancy Farmer said she'd caught Becky at it… if Nancy was telling the truth and not just expressing her disdain for the girl.

To hear that kind of description once, you could say it was envy or disdain. Twice and it might well be hearsay, but three times and (at least as far as I was concerned) it was the truth.

"And her parents never realised what she was up to – or down to – when their back was turned?" I asked.

"I think they did, but they wouldn't wanna hear it. God botherers, Chrissy. I mean, don't get me wrong, there's nothing wrong with having your religion, but you shouldn't let it blind you to what your brats are playing at." Before I could reply, Linda went on. "I can read your mind. Because her folks were away for the weekend – some kind of gospel gathering in Mablethorpe as I remember – you think that Becky took someone back to their place, changed her mind and he strangled her then killed the dog. That would let Prater nicely off the hook, but I'm sorry, girl, it didn't happen. Jacko Prater thought the place was empty, broke in, mashed the dog, Becky caught him out, and he throttled her."

It made a sort of sense... or rather, it would have done if I didn't know different.

"I have a serious problem with that, Linda. Look, we both know Jack Prater. Yeah, he's been known to thump the odd householder who caught him the act, so we know he's not afraid to lash out, but Becky was strangled. That takes time, and on every occasion when Jacko was caught on the job, he landed out and ran for it. Why go the whole hog this time, why spend more time killing her than it would take to just lamp her? Why run the risk of a life sentence rather than a couple of years for burglary, why, why, why, when he could have just punched her lights out and run for it? It doesn't make any sense."

"And if he's so innocent, why cough to it when he was questioned?"

Several answers sprang to mind, but none of them were convincing, and the front runner – coercion – was unpalatable. But Prater had hinted at it when he suggested the police never looked at their own officers?

A smug look on her face, Linda was waiting for me to answer her (technically) rhetorical question. I obliged. "You know something? That's an excellent question." She didn't pick up my hint, so I reserved any further comment.

"So where are you up to with your inquiries?" she asked.

"Not very far," I admitted. "When we got back from Wealstun on Saturday, Eric and I were arrested and charged for withholding information."

She chuckled. "So it's personal now, is it?"

"It's personal," I agreed. "I've spoken to Elaine Anguage and her kids, and I called at Springer's where Becky used to work. Spoke to Mr Brian Springer and one Nancy Farmer."

Linda laughed again. "Mr wonderful and miss glamourpuss."

The comment caused my eyebrows to rise.

Linda checked her watch. "Twenty-five past three. I'm due back on in about five minutes, Chrissy. Just time to tell you that we went through all that when Becky was first killed. Only after we'd nicked and charged Prater, mind. At that time, Brian's dad, Irwin Springer, ran the company, and he was another dyed-in-the-wool churchgoer. The same chapel as the Walmers, as it happens, which is how Becky got her job."

I tutted. "There's nothing wrong with faith, Linda. I go to church myself now and then." I silently admitted to myself that it was more then than now.

"I didn't say there was, but you shouldn't let it dominate your life the way the Walmers do, the way Irwin Springer and his missus did. Anyway, like I said, that's how Becky got her job." She giggled again. She always did have an excellent sense of humour. "If old Irwin knew about her larking around with anything in pants, he'd have kicked her out, and so would her parents. Anyway, at that time, Brian Springer had a bit of a rep for putting it about, and we did pick up a rumour that he and Nancy Farmer were getting it on. And he was married at the time."

"Interesting. He came across as all very faithful Mr happily married when I spoke to him."

"Well, he wouldn't, wouldn't he? Any fella would."

"And any woman," I added with my thoughts hovering around the ten minutes I spent with Ms Farmer. "Did Springer try it on with Becky, do you know?"

She got to her feet. "Haven't a clue, but it wouldn't surprise me. His missus was pregnant at the time. In fact, she was in the maternity ward giving birth on the night Becky was topped. Regardless, he won't have been getting much at home in the run up to the daughter's birth, will he? Listen, Chrissy, I'll have to get back to the job. It's been great seeing you. Why don't we get together for a beer or three one night?"

"I'll bell you when Dennis lets me off the leash," I said. I didn't mean it. Linda always drank more heavily than me, and given her girth, it didn't look as if she'd eased up to accommodate middle age.

We parted company, Linda back to her patrols, me out into the rain, scurrying to my car.

Throwing off the hood of my coat, I started the engine and sat there, waiting for the heater to send me warm messages.

Like everyone else, Linda was adamant that

135

they got it right when they charged Prater, but tiny holes were beginning to appear in the story.

First, Brian Springer. He lied to me when he said he was with his wife at Jumping Jacks that night. How could he be if she was in the maternity wing of Haxford Cottage Hospital?

Then there was the presence of Kitson and Penning at the scene. In a murder investigation, the sequence of events is quite rigid. When someone calls in, uniforms go out and check that it's not a prank call. The initial call from uniform would be to Haxford station, and local CID should have got there first to secure the scene properly. On confirmation of a suspicious death, Haxford would then call senior CID officers, and forensics. In Haxford, the SIO and scientific support would come from Huddersfield. So how come Kitson and Penning were there before Paddy and Linda?

Could it be that Kitson and/or Penning knew in advance, and could it be that one of them had embedded the incriminating thread into Becky's fingernail?

It was an unlikely but not unheard of scenario, and if it was anything like true it meant that a) one of them had been bought and b) he knew who the real killer was. Giving the matter some wider thought, it could actually have been one of them. If so, Kitson was favourite when I considered his attitude to women.

This train of thought merely opened up another question.

Why had Prater confessed? He had a record stretching back to his teens and he wasn't stupid.

Notwithstanding that single and damning piece of evidence – the thread – there was no way that he would have voluntarily owned up to a crime he hadn't committed. How had Kitson or Penning persuaded him to confess?

Any number of methods offered themselves up, but whether soft – own up, Jacko, and we'll make sure your missus and kids are taken care of – or hard – take it on board, Jacko, or it'll be bad news for your missus and kids – it was still coercion.

I don't know how long I sat there mulling the possibilities, but I knew when I pulled away and made for home, that I would have to take this to Mandy or Paddy. No prizes for guessing my preference.

I needn't have worried. When I pulled into the drive, Mandy's car was parked there waiting for me.

Chapter Twelve

"Do you know how much trouble you've caused?" Mandy asked.

"And do you know how glad I am to hear that?" I placed two beakers of coffee on the kitchen table.

Notwithstanding the pleasant half hour or so that I spent with Linda, I was in a brass tacks mood and even Cappy the Cat realised it when I let us into the house. After pretending to be pleased to see us, a couple of bitten off words from me persuaded him it was safer to get out of the way, and he disappeared into the front room. If Mandy hadn't worked out my mood by then, she would in the next few minutes.

Taking a seat opposite her, I waded in. "I have evidence – not proof – but evidence that Jack Prater was framed for Becky Walmer's murder. Rather than focussing on that, you and Paddy went over the top arresting and reporting Eric and me."

I'd known Mandy too long to imagine that she would just knuckle under. "You were in the wrong, Chrissy. It's debatable whether you should have watched that video, but you should have brought it to us, not shown it to Reitman."

"I'm aware of that. I know it might technically be an offence, but you still went too far, and as a result, Eric was hauled over the coals and I've been fired."

Rather than respond to my allegations, she digressed. "Fired? How can you be? You're self-employed."

"Another technicality. Radio Haxford have terminated my contract, and I'll have a fight on my hands to make them pay what they owe me, so don't expect me to feel any sympathy for the problems I've created. Note; problems and created, not trouble and caused."

On the news that my radio contract was terminated, her face fell. We had been friends for so long that no matter how much we disagreed or argued, I knew her sympathy was genuine. "Oh hell. I'm sorry. If it had just been me, I would have let it go with a warning, but Paddy was with us, and you did goad him. As it hap—"

I cut her off. "And we both know why." Again I didn't give her time to get a word in. "Because he's so in love with the legend that was Kitson that he couldn't bear to think that he might have been bent. A legend? More like a leg end from all I've been hearing."

Whatever she had been going to say, Mandy forgot about it and fought back. "Come on, Chrissy. When it came to the job, Kitson was straight as a dye. We all know that."

"Except that in this case, I don't believe he was. I've been talking to Linda Risley, and without realising it, she posed a serious question." I paused so that the impact of my query would strike home full force. "Explain this: how come Kitson and Frank Penning got to the Walmers' place before

139

Paddy and Linda?"

Mandy was about to drink from her beaker, but my words stopped her mid-slurp. "What?"

From there, I went through my meeting with Linda and the deductions which came from it, including Brian's Springer's lie about his wife's whereabouts. Mandy, was more interested in Kitson and Penning's pre-emptive appearance at the scene.

"He and Penning were based in Huddersfield," I said, "and fair comment, they were the obvious people to lead the investigation, but uniformed must have rung Haxford station, and technically, Paddy, Linda, and whoever else was in CID should have been there before anyone from Huddersfield, and they would have rung in asking for senior officers. Linda assured me that when she and Paddy got there, Kitson and Penning were already on site, kicking their heels waiting for forensics and the pathologist. Now how did that happen, Mandy?"

She suddenly became my old friend, the determined detective. "I don't know, but I'll make it my business to find out." A moment of hesitation. "It might be that there's a simple explanation."

"Like they were already in Haxford on another call? True, but even so, Haxford station wouldn't have contacted them. They'd have called local CID first, and when Paddy and Linda or whoever else reported, they would have got onto Huddersfield who would have roped in Kitson and Penning. Get Paddy to sort that one out." Once more, I pressed home the attack. "You're looking for an escape route, and there isn't one... at least not one that springs to mind. You've been at this game long enough to know better. First on the scene are uniformed, then local CID, and if it needs to go higher, they put the call through to Division."

Mandy held up her hands in surrender. "Right, right, I get the picture." She made an effort to calm down again. "It still doesn't mean they framed Prater, and it doesn't explain why he coughed to the job."

She took a large swallow of coffee, put her cup down and gazed around my kitchen. I half expected her to tell me it needed a bit of redecoration (Dennis had been trying to cook again and the wallpaper above the cooker was showing signs of the strain).

Cappy the Cat, obviously taking the brief silence to indicate a truce, paid us a visit, and Mandy cooed over him for a minute, during which he looked at me as if to say, 'You're my head servant and this is how you should be treating me, not kicking me out of your way', but when she made no greater effort to feed him than I did, he took the hump again, and disappeared.

When she next spoke, Mandy was in a more conciliatory mood. "I came here to see what you might be able to tell me, Chrissy, so just to bring you up to speed and as I tried to tell you a minute or two back, Paddy didn't push those reports through against you and Reitman. He's marked them down as a verbal. Then he set me and your Simon the task of going over the Becky Walmer case. Do you know how much paperwork there is on it? When I moaned about it, Paddy told me to get on with but he also asked me to speak to you, see if you're willing to help. Y'see? He's taking it seriously, having his doubts, and by rights, what you've just pointed out to me should have occurred to him twenty years ago."

"He was probably too much in awe of Kitson."

"Probably." She began to plead. "Come on, Chrissy. You must know more than you're letting on. I've never seen you so worked up over a case."

Listening to her, learning that Paddy had not charged either Eric or me, I began to calm down at last, and when I answered, I was placider. Or should that be more placid? I really should invest in a new dictionary.

"I've had a lot on my mind just lately. I'm sunk at Radio Haxford. If we want to be brutally honest, the mystery hour was probably doomed before ever it got under way, Lost Friends is running out of steam, and I have Dennis constantly checking the smart meter and harping on about the price of gas and electricity. Then I got that email which turned out to be from a serving police officer – and don't look like that, Mandy. I didn't know. I mean, I wouldn't know Tyndall from a hole in the road, and for all I knew, the video could have been a set up; staged. A clever bit of work from one of Prater's buddies. But to get an email and video like that, to learn that our own police were possibly guilty of a cover-up all those years ago… well, it got to me. You and Paddy made matters worse on Saturday, and Langdon piled the agony on when he tried to shut me up."

"Langdon?" Her query was another distraction designed to calm me down again.

"James Langdon. The big boss. Controller at

142

Radio Haxford. He ordered me and Eric to drop it. Eric works for them so he has no choice, but as you pointed out, I'm self-employed and I told him to get knotted. He tore up my contract and as I said, he's refusing to pay me." I sighed. "I'll see what comes of it and if he won't poppy up, I'll talk to our Stephen."

"Right. So we're the bad guys along with Radio Haxford. But even so, you've been out and about over the last few days. You must know more than you're letting on." When I hesitated, she pressed again. "Come on, Chrissy. We're the dream team, remember. We nailed the Graveyard Poisoner, didn't we?"

To be pedantic, I was the one who pinned down the Graveyard Poisoner. Mandy just tagged along for the final confrontation. I didn't say so. Instead, I said, "I don't know anything, but I do have strong suspicions, and they don't include Jack Prater."

"Good. Then let me have them and we'll compare notes."

So I told her about everyone I had seen and spoken to since the issue first blew up. Most of it was not news to her, as she said when I was through.

"Kitson and Penning knew about Becky Walmer's rep for being easy at the time. It's in the case file, but they discounted it when they found the evidence against Prater. However, there's no mention of Brian Springer's bed-hopping activities, nor about his wife just giving birth. They did speak to him, but all they got was the same guff you got from him. Something to do with the company's

143

Easter thrash at Jumping Jacks and his wife did confirm it. The same goes for Nancy Farmer. Beyond that, Elaine Anguage gave a statement insisting that Jacko was down south at the time and came home wallowing in cash, but given her past, no one gave her any cred."

"And of course, Prater never told anyone where he was down south."

"If what Tyndall said is the truth, it's not surprising, is it?"

I agreed right away. "Jacko said Kitson had no evidence on him for the Walmer killing, so he kept his mouth shut during the early interview."

I felt the frustration rising again. Circumstantial evidence, hearsay and opinion. That was all I had. The word of two lifelong criminals, a woman with a history of prostituting herself and whose word could not be relied upon, the coincidental arrival of two officers at the crime scene who shouldn't have been there at that time, all set against the word of that long-serving police officer who could boast an exemplary (not counting his sexual harassment) record.

"You haven't spoken to Frank Penning?" Mandy asked.

"I haven't got round to it yet. Besides, I don't see the point. Think about it. Assuming this was all a setup, it could have been either Kitson or Penning. If I see Penning, he'll only lie about it. In any case, I don't have an address or phone number for him."

"I can get you those."

That threw me. "Yes... but... Well, surely now you're taking the case more seriously—"

144

She cut in. "Thing is, Chrissy – and this comes from Paddy, not just me – if we go in, Penning will hide behind every rule in the book. He'll confuse the issue so much we won't know our P's from our Q's. If you go see him, he'll feel much more confident. Plus, you can pressure him in ways that we can't. Plus, as you're doing it with our blessing, you know for a fact that we won't hassle you afterwards. You see?"

I wouldn't let her have it that easy. "I haven't forgotten what Paddy said to that DCI Rothman in Cambridge. Rothman quoted it verbatim. According to him, Paddy's precise words were, 'keep that nosy old bat away from your inquiries'. That's not exactly going out of his way to encourage me, is it?"

"Aw, come on. That's just Paddy. We all know what he's like. The truth is, Chrissy, he's insecure. Mind, with a wife like Janine, it's hardly surprising. If he opens his mouth to yawn she's on his case. Truth is, he thinks a lot of you and he recognises your abilities. He won't say so because he likes to be in control of inquiries and he doesn't want to appear as if he's letting go of that control. But he's not stupid, and you know he isn't. He can see the advantages of using someone like you to achieve a result he knows he won't get.

She was almost begging me to agree, and I was on the point of capitulation, but I never got to say anything. My smartphone beeped to announce an incoming text message and I read it.

Remember what happened to your old man last year? It could be worse next time. Mind your own bloody business.

145

As I read it, Mandy went on. "All we need you to do is wind Penning up. Yeah? If we tried it, he'd tie us in procedural knots but if he – or Kitson for that matter – really was guilty of a cover up, and he thinks you're gonna lay it at his door, he'll open up."

"Either that or he'll take out a tin opener and open me up." I laid the phone on the table and turned it to face Mandy so she could read it.

Mandy's variable features underwent another change, and I could sense the anger building in her. "It's beginning to look more and more as if you're right about Prater." Her hand shook (with anger, I assumed) as she made a note of the sender's number. "I don't suppose it'll do us a ha'pporth of good, but I'll get our guys to chase up the source and the transmission mast. Ten to one it'll be an unregistered phone, but we'll have a go."

I took my phone back, forwarded the message to Dennis and then rang him. In keeping with the mood of the last few days, he wasn't pleased to hear from me, but I eventually got him to shut up and listen to me.

"I've had a threat over the phone, and it's aimed at you. I've just forwarded the text to you so you know what I'm talking about. Now listen to me, Dennis, whatever you do, make sure you're never left alone in that workshop. Make sure Tony, Lester or Greg are with you at all times."

"You know, life'd be a lot simpler if you stopped poking your nose into stuff."

"Yes, but it wouldn't be half so much fun. Bear in mind what I've said, Dennis."

I ended the call and concentrated on Mandy. "At least you're coming round to my way of thinking. This text is telling me to back off the Prater enquiry, and why would anyone threaten me or Dennis unless there's something fishy about it?"

"I did say you're preaching to the choir," she said. "Paddy's not happy about any of it and we know what he's like. He bends the rules so far, anyone would think they're made of rubber, but the one thing he can't stand is a bent cop. Yes, we're with you, Chrissy, and as of now, I'm interested in who could have sent this, so come on, tell me what you've got."

I didn't have to think for too long. "There aren't many candidates. James Langdon, Brian Springer, and Nancy Farmer. They're the only three who spring to mind. It can't be Elaine Anguage. She's still insistent that Prater is innocent. If it's anyone other than those three, then the interested party has had a tip off from one of them." I drummed irritated fingers on the table. "The only ones who know the truth are Kitson and Penning."

"And whoever killed Becky... assuming it wasn't Prater. Talking of whom, by the way, we've had a call from his lawyer. She's appealing on the grounds of unsafe conviction. That's one step away from having his sentence quashed and a massive bill for compensation. I'm not blaming you, Chrissy, but you've opened a can of worms—"

"Which needed opening," I cut in.

"Which, fair comment, needed opening, but I dread to think where the repercussions will end." She took out her phone. "Let me just get Penning's address and number and get a track on this text."

Five minutes later, she had the necessary information which she passed to me, and Mandy made ready to leave. She checked her watch. "Bit late in the day for today, I think. Are you recording tomorrow?"

I shrugged. "As far as I'm concerned, no. I told you, Langdon fired me. All I have left with Radio Haxford is agony aunt and that's live every Tuesday." I picked up the beakers and moved them to the sink for washing up. "If I'm free, I'll chase Penning up first thing tomorrow. If I get a call from Reitman that nothing's changed, it'll be Thursday."

"Thanks, Chrissy, and by the way, it's great to be on the same side."

Chapter Thirteen

Matters between Dennis and me showed no hint of improvement, and after our evening meal he took himself into the front room to watch his motor car programmes, I dealt with the dishes, and then moved to the conservatory to watch the sun set behind a turbulent sky which reflected my inner agitation.

As far as I was concerned, the threatening message confirmed that Prater had indeed been framed for Becky Walmer's murder. If there were ever any doubts, that text dispelled them.

Far from feeling vindicated, it left me anxious, even frightened. Not so much for myself but for Dennis. Recent arguments aside, he was my husband, and I cared about him, and even though I'd warned him to make sure he was never left alone in the workshop, I knew it would happen one day. Lester was away early every day. His philosophy of work was a job that would make him enough money to keep him in beer and tobacco. Tony and Greg were more like Dennis. They worked longer hours, but neither of them were driven the way my old man was, and one evening, sooner or later, they would go, Dennis would be alone and this hidden, evil creature (or the people who carried out his orders) would seize the opportunity.

Who was he? I kept coming back to the same question. Of the three names I had thrown at Mandy, James Langdon was favourite. Of that trio, he was the only one who had ordered me to drop my investigation. Neither Springer nor Nancy Farmer appeared concerned about my activities, and both talked freely enough, albeit only in general (or in Nancy's case derogatory) terms. Then I remembered that as I sat outside Springer's office, he was arguing with overalls and rigger boots. Coincidence? The builder complaining? Or was O & RB connected to the crime? A man paid to do the dirty work? I'd assured Springer that I was not investigating, merely researching Becky's background, so if he was in cahoots with O & RB, it meant he did not believe me. It also meant he knew more than he had told me, and of course, he did lie about being with his wife in Jumping Jacks.

Mandy summed it up right, Kitson and Penning held the key to this appalling crime... both appalling crimes; Becky's murder and the framing of Jack Prater. Kitson was out of bounds for me. A private eye I might be, but I couldn't afford to go flying off to Spain to grill him. Aside from throwing a fit at the cost, Dennis would insist on coming with me. Oh yes, tight-fisted he might be, but he liked soaking up the sun (and beer) on the Costa del Sol when the opportunity arose.

I therefore assumed that Paddy and Mandy would deal with Kitson, which left me, as Mandy had requested, with Penning. As the gloomy daylight faded, I looked up his address on Google Maps. North and west of Huddersfield town centre it didn't look too difficult to find. I didn't know him, he probably didn't know me, but I was determined that he would by ten o'clock tomorrow morning.

Eric rang just after half past seven and begged

me to reconsider my decision.

"It wasn't my decision," I countered. "It was Langdon's. He tore my contract up."

"He tore up a photocopy of your contract, Chrissy, and as long as you're willing to co-operate, toe the line, and we can do something with the mystery hour, I'm sure I can get him to reconsider."

"I said no, I meant no, and after today, I'm even more determined to prove Jack Prater innocent."

"Why? What happened?"

"I'm sorry, Eric, I can't tell you. It's under legal wraps, but it virtually confirms that Prater was railroaded." As I spoke, I recalled the bitter interlude with Langdon. "You know, I've been thinking about it, and I got the impression that Langdon has his own agenda for wanting me to drop the case and it has nothing to do with the rubbish ratings for Christine Capper's Mystery Hour or making Radio Haxford look bad. If the programme was that bad, he'd have dropped it weeks ago. Whatever the real situation, you could do me a favour. The next time you see him, tell him what I've just told you. I know Prater is innocent and I'm making it my business to prove it, and when I do, I will go public on everything, including the way he tried to shut me up."

"That would risk upsetting a lot of influential people."

"Turn that proposition on its head and ask yourself, doesn't it matter that at least one influential person is upsetting me by trying to suppress the truth? Trust me on this, Eric, your common or garden Haxforder will come down on my side more than theirs. Now, if you'll excuse me, I have a lot to think about."

I cut the call before he could say another word and sank into my thoughts again.

Not that turning the problem over and over in my head did any good. I would need someone, somewhere to break the veil of silence, and for all Mandy's entreaties, I couldn't see Penning giving us that much.

Was there anyone else I might put pressure on? Springer? Farmer? Brian Springer was a non-starter. He was like Langdon; master of his own domain and he wouldn't budge. Nancy Farmer had probably been told to button it, especially if there was any truth in the rumour of an affair between her and the aforementioned Mr Springer.

Dennis came into the conservatory just before eight o'clock. "Are you just gonna sit here all night?"

"I've a lot on my mind."

"Aye, and don't we all know it?" Before I could rise to the bait, he tried to tempt me. "There's a Midsomer wossnames on the telly. One of your favourite episodes."

"In which case, Dennis, I must have seen it before, so I'll give it a miss. Besides, I'll have enough TV to watch on Saturday during the coronation."

"Yeah, well, I'll be working. But I'm on about tonight, and—"

I cut him off. "I told you, I've a lot of thinking to do."

"Yeah, but it's freezing in here. You'll catch

your death."

"I'll put the heating on if I have to."

"I thought we'd talked about that. No central heating until after nine at night, when we go back on off-peak rates."

"Agreements are made for breaking. If you don't believe me, ask James Langdon."

His face clouded with mystery. "Who's he?"

"The boss of Radio Haxford. He fired me this morning. Tore the contract up in front of me."

"Happen I should give him a medal."

He didn't wait for the obligatory backlash, but turned and left the room. As if I didn't have enough on my plate.

When I first told Dennis of the contract with Radio Haxford, he was over the moon. He had similar visions as me: stardom, pots of money, enough to expand the Haxford Fixers' business, maybe even a move from Bracken Close to somewhere more upmarket, although for the life of me I couldn't think of anywhere in Haxford which was better than Bracken Close and even if there were such places, I don't think I wanted to move to them.

These days, he loathed the idea of me working on the radio. Perhaps he really did believe I was having an affair with Eric or Reggie Monk. Well, maybe not Reggie. His BO and halitosis would automatically disbar him, and Dennis knew how fussy I was about such things (prissy, he called it). My husband visited the dentist every six months, cleaned his teeth twice a day, and he always used plenty of deodorants to dispel the smell of oil, petrol, diesel, and honest sweat.

Eric, Reggie, any other man, Dennis knew for certain that I was not, never had been, never would be unfaithful to him, so whatever his beef, I knew it would soon blow over.

Right at that moment, however, I could have lived without him acting up. I needed a break in the Prater case, and despite Mandy's optimism, I didn't see Frank Penning providing it.

It was gone eleven o'clock and I was feeling the chill by the time I left the conservatory for the warmer air of the front room, only to find the place in darkness. Dennis had gone to bed and Cappy the Cat had gone with him.

For all the hours that I sat in solitude, the thought of my shattered radio career barely crossed my mind. It was all Prater, Walmer, Prater, Walmer, and who might really be behind that girl's murder. I moved to the bathroom and got ready to join my husband and turncoat tomcat (I say that because other than at mealtimes, Cappy the Cat tended to avoid Dennis). While I washed away the grime of a long and largely fruitless day, I recalled the day Reggie Monk approached me in Terry's and asked me to take on the role of agony aunt. I was petrified at the prospect and I used every excuse I could dream up to dissuade him. Reggie was made of sterner stuff and he eventually persuaded me.

From there, my credits soon grew. Eric came up with the idea of Lost Friends after I went looking for an old flame of Hazel McQuarrie's and put out an announcement during one of my agony aunt sessions (I did find him). It was an immediate success but its popularity began to wane after Christmas and New Year.

By then, however, Eric, who was charged with bringing new programme ideas to the station, talked me into Christine Capper's Mystery Hour. I was terrified at that prospect, too, but this time it was because I had to deliver the debut programme live and in front of an audience.

I got used to it. You do. My comfort zones expanded accordingly and now, a year on from that first agony aunt session, I was quite comfortable in the studio or recording in my conservatory or speaking live before an audience. It had become a part of me. And putting aside all the moans and groans from the crew (it's cold in our house) Dennis (I was a slave to them) and even me (the team cost me a fortune in tea bags and biscuits) I enjoyed it; enjoyed the camaraderie of the crew, the modest fame, being recognised by more and more people when I was out and about, and the double standards of my neighbours, whining over the disturbance every Wednesday but secretly pleased to be living so close to someone famous-ish. I loved being a radio personality.

And now I had lost it.

Not, I would insist, through any fault of my own, but because I would not bow to pressure and throw my principles in the dustbin.

Staring at my face in the mirror as I applied a little night moisturiser, it dawned on me that Radio Haxford was not the only radio station in West Yorkshire. I don't mean it was the first time I'd ever realised it. I mean it sort of thrust itself into the forefront of my mind while I was looking at myself.

Radio Leeds, Radio Sheffield sprang into my mind. And didn't Huddersfield have its own commercial station. Good heavens, there were plenty of local radio setups across the moors in Manchester, although quite what those ex-Lancastrians (in case you've been emulating Rip van Winkle and sleeping for the last half century, they really are ex-Lancastrians. They've had their own county since about 1974) would make of a Yorkie and a woman to boot chatting to them, I don't know.

As I killed the bathroom light, made my way into the bedroom, shooed a reluctant and mutinous Cappy the Cat from my pillow, I vowed to put a CV together first thing in the morning and send it off to a few stations.

It was a few minutes shy of midnight when I doused the bedside lamp and waited for sleep to overtake me. That's when I remembered I had to go to Huddersfield first thing to harass Frank Penning.

The CV would have to wait.

***

The terraced streets in the Longwood area of Huddersfield were similar to those in many older areas of Haxford, those parts which sprang up with the Industrial Revolution and the mechanisation of the wool industry, areas where the houses were built of stone, not brick, the white mortar of the freshly pointed joints standing out in the morning sunshine.

Not that they were unbecoming. Far from it. I

156

grew up in a similar house and the modernisation process which had been ongoing since the early 1970s saw the interiors as warm, comfortable and welcoming as any 1930s-built bungalow. Well, maybe not quite. You would have to go a long way to find a place as smart and desirable as ours, and by a long way, I mean a long way from Bracken Close or Haxford or Huddersfield or maybe even Great Britain. That, of course, was my doing. Note: not Dennis. If I left it to him, the house would look like a second workshop and it would bring down the property values of the entire street. I'd often said that in such a situation, the neighbours would get up a petition demanding that we move.

Dennis left for work at half past seven most mornings, but when I crawled out of bed at quarter past, he had already gone. Anything to avoid the danger of having to speak to me, I guessed.

I wasn't unduly troubled. I was too tired to worry about it for one thing. And that's an understatement. The way I felt was closer to exhaustion.

I struggled through a light breakfast of cereal and coffee and then gave the Radio Haxford crew until 9:30 to show their faces. They didn't. No one rang either, and that tolled the death knell of my brief career.

I was tempted to ring them, but I resisted. It might send out the wrong signals; i.e. I was ready to compromise. It might also hint that I cared about my infant radio career. I did, but I didn't want them to think that. So instead, I climbed into the Diablo and set off for Longwood.

157

It was less than ten miles but awkward to get to. Awkward? It was on a similar level to Dennis and Cappy the Cat working as a double act. It was bitty, turn here, turn there, get across this busy junction, fight your way round that busy roundabout. And the stop-start progress was hampered by my fatigue. At one point I almost nodded off to sleep while waiting for a double set of traffic lights to change in my favour.

I finally pulled up outside Penning's place at ten o'clock, dragged my weary bones out of the car and rang the bell. Then knocked, then rang the bell again, then hammered on the door so loud that his neighbour, a Nora Batty look-alike, came out to see what the fuss was about.

"Is he home?"

"Hanged if I know, but he should be. He don't go anywhere on a Tuesday normally."

"It's Wednesday."

"Aye, right, it is. Well he don't go anywhere on a Wednesday either. Norrat this hour, anyroad."

I thanked her and she went back in grumbling about 'noisy beggars'. At least, I think that's what she said.

I knocked the door another couple of times, then moved along to the window. The house was on the sunward, south-facing side of the street and it was impossible to see anything of the inside without pressing my face up against the glass, and even then I had to shade my eyes with a hand over my forehead.

I still couldn't see much, but what I did see made me wish I hadn't bothered.

Frank Penning (I assumed it was him) lay dead in front of the hearth. He had to be dead. No one with his neck crooked so far to one side could possibly be alive.

Chapter Fourteen

The main police station in Huddersfield stood just off the town centre bypass close to the junction with the A62, the main route to Manchester in the days before the trans-Pennine motorway. Not that I was old enough to remember those days, but the legend is well established. My dad used to tell tales of the days when those lorries crossed Standedge in convoy. I'd never actually worked out how he knew about them. Before he retired, he spent his entire working life in Haxford.

Sat in an interview room, my temper deteriorating with each passing minute, fatigue threatening to put me to sleep at any moment, it seemed incredible to me that I had been pressed into the back of a patrol car and driven here from Longwood. They wouldn't even let me drive myself, and the Diablo was still parked outside the late Sergeant Penning's house.

When I realised Penning's situation, I dialled 999 immediately and asked for both an ambulance (in case I had it wrong and he was still alive) and the police. The local uniforms turned up first.

While I waited for them, I rattled Nora Batty's door, and half expected her to come out brandishing a sweeping brush to shoo me away. She didn't but her face was set in something close to Armageddon.

I explained the situation and asked if she'd seen any unusual activity the previous evening or this morning.

"Have I heck as like. What do you think I am? Some nosy ha'pporth? Well I'm not. I keep meself to meself. Me and me husband."

Earlier, she assured me that Penning did not venture out of the house on Tuesdays or Wednesday morning. How did she know? There was only one way, and if that didn't qualify her as a nosy ha'pporth, I don't know what would.

Within ten minutes of my call, and while I was still debating with Nora Batty, two patrol cars arrived and a team of four uniforms climbed out.

"Mrs Capper?" one of the women asked, and when I nodded, she went, "You're to come with us."

"What? Where?"

"Headquarters."

"Hang on, hang on. There's a dead man in there." I waved a wild arm at the door... unfortunately, it was Nora Batty's door and she took instant umbrage.

"There's no one dead in here."

The uniform ignored her and spoke to me. "We'll deal with that, but you're coming with us."

"No way."

"It's either that or we arrest you."

And that was it. A couple of minutes later, while the remaining officers took an enforcer (the official description of the handheld solid steel battering ram they used to break down doors) to gain access to Penning's house, I was driven off to the centre of Huddersfield, given a cup of canteen tea and left to my own devices in a tiny interview room not dissimilar to the one where Eric and I spoke with Prater.

I must have been there for an hour before two familiar faces walked in. I'd never met either man before, but I had seen them. "Detective Inspector Knock On and Detective Sergeant Block Heel," I announced. "You're a long way from your patch."

"Indeed we are, Mrs Capper. And, by the way, it's Detective *Chief* Inspector Nocton."

"And my name is Bentil."

Round one to me. I goaded, they reacted.

Taking in both of them with my icy stare, I pushed further. "Hasn't anyone told you? Your sort aren't welcome here?"

It sort of backfired on me.

Nocton glanced at his Asian sergeant, then glared at me. "I don't approve of racism, madam."

Oops. That aspect hadn't occurred to me. And Nocton wasn't alone in his repugnance. I didn't approve of racism either. "No, look, I'm sorry. You misunderstood me. When I said, 'your sort', I wasn't referring to your sergeant's ancestry. I meant you're both southerners. This is Yorkshire." It crossed my mind to say that we didn't care for anyone from south of Watford, but in my case, it wouldn't be true. I could get on with anyone from anywhere. Even Lancashire. Instead, I said, "In any case, shouldn't you be in London guarding the king for his coronation?"

"Not our job," Bentil grumbled. "We're just humble plods."

Neither of them appeared appeased, and Nocton made a point of stressing his control. "We're here, madam, and you'll have to put up with us. Now—"

I cut him off and raised my voice. "So why am I here? Why was I all but arrested at Frank Penning's place? What am I supposed to have done wrong? Because as far as I'm concerned, I haven't—"

"You're not under arrest, Mrs Capper," the inspector interrupted, "and you're not under caution, and you are not here for interrogation. You're helping with our inquiries."

I made to stand up. "In that case—"

"But you won't be going anywhere until we're through talking."

And that was the final straw. I stood, leaned on my arms, the fists balled on the table for support, all in a half-hearted attempt to dominate them. "Do you know who you're dealing with? I'm Christine Capper. Ex-cop, private eye, blogger, vlogger and a radio star…"

Oh my goodness. Did I really say that? Again?

"Sit down, Mrs Capper."

I disregarded Bentil's instruction and played on my celebrity (yuk) persona. "I eat people like you for breakfast."

He wasn't impressed. "Sit down, Mrs Capper. Otherwise, I will come round the table and make you sit down."

The sergeant was quite calm. He was also quite big and fit and I knew he would carry through his threat if I didn't toe the line. I sat down.

Nocton took the lead. "We spoke to James

Langdon at Radio Haxford earlier and he assured us that your contract with them has been terminated. So let's a have little less of the big I am, eh? It serves only to make you look slightly ridiculous, and frankly, madam, no matter what your status, real or imaginary, it's of no interest to us. Your activities, however, are."

Determined to be as uncooperative as I could, I said. "I want a cup of tea. Milk, no sugar." I was sulking, in a worse mood than I could remember for some time.

Nocton nodded at his sidekick, and Bentil left the room to organise it.

While I waited, I debated whether it was worth my while trying to push the inspector. Probably not. Detectives worked in pairs. That way they had back up for everything that was said and done. It was the same reason they advised suspects to have a solicitor present, but it has to be said that (legal advice aside) the system was largely redundant in this day and age of audio and video recordings.

There again, Nocton had been at pains to point out that I was not under arrest, nor was I under caution, and he had not offered me a lawyer. Furthermore, neither he nor his partner had touched the recording equipment.

"What about my activities?"

"When Sergeant Bentil returns. For now, let me reassure you that these are general inquiries. Depending on the outcome of them, we may decide to press charges."

"While leaving Jack Prater to rot in jail."

Nocton gave me a bleak, insincere smile. "That

is none of my concern." He seemed to relax a little. "Langdon wasn't the only one I spoke to about you. I had a long chat with DI Quinn. He speaks very highly of you."

It's a good job I didn't have a cuppa. I would have spilled it or choked on it. Paddy Quinn speaking well of me? No wonder the weather was so quirky.

Nocton went on. "According to him, you're a nuisance but you have a knack of getting to the right answers, usually by the most circuitous of routes. He credits you with helping him and his team to solve several cases in the Huddersfield area."

"Haxford," I said.

"I beg your pardon?"

"Haxford. It's about seven or eight miles south of Huddersfield and it's where I live and work. I thought you might have worked it out having spoken to Radio Haxford."

"Ah. I'm sorry. I didn't."

Bentil returned, placed disposable cups before each of us, then took out his notebook as Nocton went into the more formal part of proceedings.

"A little over a week ago, you received an anonymous email with a video file attached. That video was part of a confidential police interview, on the back of which an IOPC investigation is likely to take place, as well as possible criminal proceedings against a number of people. Our inquiries led us to Detective Constable Ivan Jephcott. Under questioning, Jephcott admitted sending you the file. Do you deny having watched it, Mrs Capper?"

"No."

"Yet as an ex police officer, you must have understood that it was confidential. So why did you not bring it to the attention of your local police?"

My answer was the same, simple one I gave Paddy. "How was I supposed to know it was real? For all I knew, it could have been staged. Besides, I did hand it over to Paddy Quinn and Sergeant Hiscoe."

"Only after you were arrested and charged. However what you did with that file after watching it is not really my concern."

"No, you're looking to leave Prater where he is, aren't you?"

"I told you once, he is none of my concern either. No, Mrs Capper, my interest lies in your relationship with Ivan Jephcott and how many other snippets of confidential information he might have sent you."

I was astonished. "What? Have you taken leave of your senses?"

"It's a simple enough question, madam," Bentil put in.

"And the answer is simple, too. I have no relationship, as you put it, with this DC Jephcott. I never heard of him until Paddy and Mandy told me about him on Saturday, several days after I received his original email and text. And if you've checked the interview between me and the Haxford police, you'll know that my initial reaction was to dump the lot as spam. It was only when he rang me and urged me to watch the video that I did."

"And even then, you did not take it to the police."

"I had a meeting with Sergeant Hiscoe, and she told me in a roundabout way that the West Yorkshire police were sitting on Prater's case through lack of evidence. I made it my business to go out and find that evidence. And before you get out of your pram again, Mr Nocton, I did find it. Everywhere. And I found more this morning."

That got a reaction, and it was several seconds and two sips of tea before the chief inspector recovered. "You did?"

"Frank Penning. I saw him through the window. He's dead and it looked to me like he was murdered. Why? Why did James Langdon order me to drop the inquiry? Why did he discipline my friend, Eric Reitman for helping me? Why did I receive a text threatening to give my husband a good beating if I didn't mind my own business? How could Jack Prater point out one of the items stolen in the Fairburn House burglary in less than two seconds unless he was there that night? How come two detectives from Huddersfield got to the scene of Becky's murder before our local bobbies?" I paused for breath. "Someone, Mr Nocton, wants my inquiry shut down and they're willing to go to criminal lengths to ensure it. As for you and your sergeant, you might be focussed on the reputation of the police service, but I'm more interested in a miscarriage of justice which has left an innocent man in jail for the last twenty years, and a murderer free for that same length of time. And if DC Jephcott had to break the rules to bring that out into the open, then good for him. He should get a medal, not the sack. And when this is all over, when Prater is free, I'll make sure every news channel in Yorkshire, the whole flaming country knows about it." Catching my breath for the second time, I sat back. "Now if you're going to charge me, get on with it."

My diatribe took them totally by surprise and the inspector took his time before responding. "I'm not altogether sure what charges I could bring against you, madam, other than, perhaps colluding with DC Jephcott, but I have no firm evidence to support that. In other words, I accept that his communication with you came out of nowhere, but I would appreciate understanding how he tracked you down."

"Internet," I replied. "He probably just googled Haxford, private investigator. I'm the only properly trained and registered private eye in the town."

"Ah. I see. We will check on that but for the moment, you're free to go. Before we part company, however, allow me to point out that all the so-called evidence you put before me just now is circumstantial."

"I know. But for them to murder Frank Penning means I must be getting warm... assuming it is murder, of course. And talking of Penning, my car is still out at his place. Any chance you can get me back there?"

"I'll get it arranged."

I turned my attention to Sergeant Bentil. "Please accept my apologies for my stupid remark earlier. I have no truck with racism, and I didn't mean it in the way you thought."

He was charity personified. "Already forgotten,

Mrs Capper. You may not be racist, but I come across plenty of people who are, so I'm quite used to it."

Less than ten minutes later, I was in the rear seat of a patrol car on my way back to Longwood, and I was feeling quite pleased with myself. I, Christine Capper, had taken on two detectives from Scotland Yard and won my argument... after a fashion. If nothing else, I forced them to face up to Prater's innocence. Note: innocence, not alleged innocence. The events of the last twenty-four hours were enough to persuade me of it.

As I got out of the car outside Penning's place, I noticed the white van of forensics and the comings and goings of one or two people in one-piece coveralls and overshoes. I approached a uniformed constable on sentry duty.

"Definitely murdered was he?"

"Sorry, missus, not my place to say anything."

"No problem. I'll ask Paddy Quinn."

He laughed. "Knick-Knack Paddywhack? He won't tell you anything."

"Care to bet?" I held up my hand and crossed the fingers. "Like that, me and Paddy. We have been for years."

Leaving him gaping after me, I climbed into the Diablo, started the engine and took out my smartphone. I'd been compelled to switch it off while I was in the police station.

I rang Dennis first, to learn that everything was fine at Haxford Fixers. I told him what had happened to Frank Penning (I still assumed it was murder) and ordered him to be careful.

169

Then I rang Mandy and told her of my morning.

"We already know about it," she said. "Paddy was talking to those Scotland Yard bods earlier. But I'll tell you what they don't know, and I'll bet you don't either. Pete Kitson's dead."

Chapter Fifteen

It was almost two o'clock when I sat, drinking tea with Mandy in her office. I'd had no lunch and the fatigue was threatening to catch up with me again, but I had no choice. I had to know what had happened.

"We've been trying to track down Kitson for a few days, but every time we rang, we got his missus and according to her, he was out playing golf every day and liked to sink a few beers when he got back to the clubhouse. Paddy left it at that and he was going to ring back this morning, but we had a call from the Spanish police. Mrs K put them onto us. It seems that two days ago, Kitson got into a bit of an argument on the golf club car park. It turned to a fight, and you know what Kitson was like. Never one to back down, was he? One of them pulled a blade and put Kitson in hospital. He died last night."

"Have the Spanish police got them?"

Mandy shook her head. "They legged it and no one at the golf club knows who they were. Young, white males. That's it. Spanish cops have CCTV and if we need it, we'll ask for it, but right now it's not an issue because, to be honest, it could be totally unrelated. Even so, if we think about it in terms of what happened to Frank Penning and the text you

171

got yesterday, it could have been someone from Haxford. Let's face it, with a walk-on flight, you can get to Malaga in less than four hours. A quick drive down the coast, and you're on Kitson's doorstep. Do the business and get a late flight back to Manchester or Leeds and Bradford. If that's so, then someone, Chrissy, is spending a lot of money to make sure those who might know something keep it to themselves. Who do we know who's worth more than a tenner, who could spend money like that without feeling it?" She went on before I could slide my brain into thinking mode. "Brian Springer springs to mind – pun intentional."

I doubted it. "He seemed like a run-of-the-mill waste of space to me, but quite pleasant."

"Guys like that don't go around wearing a badge that say, 'I pay contract killers to sort out my troubles', and he did lie about being with his wife on the night in question."

"True, but that could be because he was with Nancy Farmer or some other willing woman."

"Like Becky Walmer?" Mandy took a wet of tea. "How did you get on with the whizz kids from Scotland Yard?"

"I clued them up on my progress – correction, *our* progress so far and they're going away happy." I chewed my lip and following her lead swilled down some tea. "Thing is, Mandy, what about Dennis and his pals? Are they seriously at risk?"

"No two ways about it. Especially Dennis. But it doesn't end there. What about Paddy and Linda Risley? Closer to home, what about you?"

That sent a shock through me and I fell back on

excuses. "That text didn't threaten me."

"No, and it didn't specifically threaten Dennis either. It mentioned what happened to him last year and said it could be worse this time. It could mean him, you, or both of you. But don't worry, Chrissy. We can get you some protection."

"You can't nursemaid me every minute of the day." I chewed my lip some more. "I'll nip over to Benny's Bargain Basement when I leave here. I'm sure he stocks pepper spray."

Mandy shook her head. "If he does, I'll have him in court tomorrow morning. Do I have to remind you that carrying pepper spray is illegal in this country?"

"Oh. Is it? Yes, of course it is. Well, what's that other stuff, the stuff that coats them in a red dye that they can't get off for days?"

"You mean Farbgel."

"That's it. And don't tell me that's illegal. I know it isn't."

"True, but it ain't cheap and hairspray is just as good."

"Yes but I can't see Harmony leaving him red in the face, except when his mates smell it on him. I'll see if Benny has any of that Fargel stuff."

"Farbgel." Mandy made a point of stressing the correct pronunciation. "If Benny doesn't have it, it must be the only thing he doesn't sell. Stick to hairspray, Chrissy. You'll leave him smelling nice and his eyes watering." She chuckled. "And remember your basic training. You know where to kick a man, don't you?"

"Where he wouldn't want to show his mother.

Most men anyway. When it comes to people like Dennis, you'd have to kick him in the wallet."

Her smile faded. "You two are not getting on any better?"

"Not so you'd notice," I confessed. "Thing is, he won't come out and say exactly what's wrong and I can't put my finger on it."

The smile returned. "Are you sure it's not cos he's not getting his finger on it often enough?"

I sniffed. "We do all right, and we're not entirely past it, you know. Besides, it's usually me who has to ask. Dennis is too busy dreaming of Ford Cortinas and Vauxhall Vivas." I dragged the subject back where it was supposed to be. "When Eric and I spoke to Prater, he was insistent that everyone in Haxford knew who really killed Becky. How many other suspects were there?"

"Serious suspects? Not many, and the moment they found that thread under her fingernail and got the DNA result, there were none."

Her answer jerked my thinking into a different traffic lane. "It's interesting, isn't it? That thread? If we're to assume it was planted, where did they get that thread? I mean it's practically certain that Kitson or Penning planted it before they arrested Prater, so where and how did they get hold of it? They must have had access to his laundry or wardrobe or something. How could they manage that?"

"If it really was them, and remember, we don't have proof of that, and think about who they were. A couple of senior detectives. They could get access to the evidence room at almost any police station at

West Yorkshire. In other words, Chrissy, that thread could have been stored as definitive evidence from one of those times where Prater really was guilty, and it's safe to say that in Becky's case, forensics won't have run an exhaustive search to ensure it hadn't come from one of those old cases, because at the time there was no suggestion of a foul."

"Tight for time, though," I said. "And risky. For both of them. If anyone caught them at it…"

"No one did, obviously."

"Suppose it wasn't them? I mean, I think they planted it, but suppose they didn't steal it from the evidence store. Suppose they didn't actually steal it at all? How else could it have been acquired?"

She shrugged. "Ask me another. Some pal of Prater's who wanted him out of the way? Someone who might have had access to Jacko's house or someone who might have called on…"

She trailed off and the way the smile crept across both our faces, I'm sure the idea occurred to us both at the same time.

"Elaine Anguage."

"Elaine Anguage."

We said it together.

"One of her punters," Mandy said.

I agreed. "To quote Dennis, her company never came free, but when they were through with business, she would have taken her time getting dressed, and that would give him the opportunity… Oh. Wait. The kids. Tommy and Wynn."

Mandy shook her head. "In Elaine's case, they were never an issue. If it was late at night, they'd be in bed, if it was during the day, then she'd shuffle them off to her mother's when she was expecting a john."

I glanced at the clock. Half past two. "Time enough to catch her and still be home in time to get Dennis's tea ready." I gulped down my tea. "I'll get over there."

Mandy finished hers. "Not on your own, you won't. You lead, I'll follow."

"Mandy, I don't need you babysitting—"

She cut me off. "Haven't we just talked about the risk to you? I'll be right behind you."

We left the police station car park together, me in the Diablo, Mandy tailgating me in a pool car. Afternoon traffic was beginning to pick up, but even so, we pulled up outside Elaine Anguage's place less than fifteen minutes later, and as we climbed out of our vehicles, so two young men came out of the house.

I was sure I recognised the one in the denim jacket and jeans, but I couldn't place him. I was also certain that I'd never seen his pal, who wore a black fleece and black jogging pants, in my life.

Denim jacket wouldn't look at me, and instead faced Mandy.

"Doing threesomes now, is she?" Mandy asked.

"Why don't you mind your own business?" black fleece argued.

Mandy flashed her warrant card. "Her activities are always my business, now scram. The pair of you." They skulked off and Mandy concentrated on me. "Something wrong, Chrissy?"

"The kid in the denim jacket. I'm sure I know him, but I can't think where from."

She giggled. "You're getting old. You've met too many people and your brain's filling up. Come on. Let's see what Elaine has to say for herself."

I let her lead the way, and she rattled the door knocker. A minute later, Elaine opened it, and it's not stretching a point to say she looked worried. That changed when she recognised Mandy.

"What do you want?"

"A word or several."

"I've nowt to say."

Mandy persisted. "We can either do it here, inside, or down at the station. Your choice, Elaine."

With a grunt and a few muttered, inaudible complaints, she let us in and closed the door behind us. Once in the shabby living room, she parked herself in an armchair and glared. "So what do you want?"

I got in before my friend. "The two men who left. Who were they?"

"Mind your own business. Nowt to do wi' you or anyone else who I have visiting."

"Yes, but—"

"She's right, Chrissy," Mandy interrupted. "Course, I could always make it my business, but that depends on how willing you are to co-operate, Elaine."

"I've asked you once what you want, and you never answered."

Mandy gave me the nod. "Jacko. He was convicted after the police found a thread from one of his cardigans or jumpers or something. We think it was planted. What we want to know is who you, er, entertained, on the night Becky Walmer was killed, because one of your punters took that thread or the garment it came from."

"Well you can bog off, can't you. I don't do names."

"Not good enough, Elaine," Mandy insisted. "You know who your johns are. You always have."

She fell silent and I pressed her. "Listen, Elaine, you've been hassling the law for the last twenty years to free Jacko. Well, this could do it. Because if the man who stole that thread wasn't the person who killed Becky, he certainly knows who did."

She was uneasy. I could see it in the way the muscles of her face worked.

"Come on Elaine," Mandy insisted. "This is your best chance to see Jacko out, free. It's what you want, isn't it?"

Still she remained silent, and I racked my tired brain to think up an angle which would make her open up to us. Tired is comparative. I was absolutely shattered, in desperate need of some sleep, and I could think of only one way to tackle her.

"Where are Teddy and Wynn?"

Her answer came back right away. "This is nothing to do with them."

"Where are they, Elaine?"

"At work. Where do you think?"

"I didn't think they had jobs. They were here the day I first came to see you."

Once again, Elaine was quick with the rebuttal. "Our Teddy works at a petrol station on Huddersfield Road and he's on afternoons. Our Wynn works as a personal shopper at CutCost. You know what I mean. Them as puts the customers' online orders together. She's on two-ten, too."

"I'll go over there and see her, see what she has to say." I stood ready to leave.

"I telled you, it's nowt to do wi' either of my kids. You just—"

"Knock it off, the pair of you," Mandy intervened before focussing on Elaine. "Now come on. We need names from you."

Elaine shook her head. "Y'see, it's awkward."

"What is?"

"Well, see, all them years ago, when I told you Jacko was home here, well, I was, like, er… lying. I never saw him that night. Happen it was him who did that girl."

Mandy's face suffused with anger, but I wasn't fooled. Not for one minute.

Mandy still beat me to the crunch. "You're telling me that you lied in court and all those times you came screaming to us, you were trying to scam Jacko out of prison. Do you know how much trouble you're…"

I tapped Mandy on the arm and she trailed off.

Now that I had the floor, I faced Elaine. "We have evidence, tons of it, that Jack is innocent, love, so let's not fool one another. He did get back here that night, and you and your kids saw him, and you've known all along that he's innocent. Instead of covering up, tell us what this rubbish is about. Is it those two men who left as we got here?"

She looked away and I turned the screws.

"You'll never be free of them, Elaine, unless you tell Mandy what the score is."

179

"Go away, both of you. Go on. Get out."

Right then Mandy's phone rang. With an irritated tut, she dug it out and put it to her ear. Elaine and I could only hear one side of the conversation but as it went on, Mandy's face became more and more serious.

She ended the call and looked on Elaine with something approaching compassion. "Maybe this'll change your mind. There's been an incident at a petrol station on Huddersfield Road. Two men attacked one of the attendants, beat seven colours out of him. I'm sorry, Elaine, but it's Teddy."

"Oh, God, no."

"He's on his way to The Cottage."

The Cottage was Haxford-ese for Haxford Cottage Hospital.

In the face of Elaine's shock, Mandy was still talking. "If you get your coat on, I'll take you there." My friend swung her attention to me. "The forecourt has CCTV and we'll be grabbing it, but at this hour, it'll likely be tomorrow before we get to it. You get off home, Chrissy, and I'll bell you first thing. And watch your back."

Chapter Sixteen

That Wednesday night would be one of the worst I could remember, not least because things between Dennis and me took a nose dive, and that started as soon as I came out of Elaine Anguage's place.

Once settled behind the wheel of the Diablo, I rang Dennis. "Teddy Anguage has been beaten up. For God's sake be careful. Make sure someone is watching your back."

"I wish you'd give over shoving your nose into stuff."

"I'm thinking of you."

"If you minded your own business, you wouldn't need to. And you can stop worrying. Grimy's put our security camera right. If anyone turns up here we'll have 'em on video."

"Wonderful. So when you're on your way to the crematorium, I'll have a video record of you being beaten to death."

"Don't talk so soft. Now is that it? Only I'm up to me neck in work as usual."

That set the mood for a night of near silence, Dennis in the front room watching his favourite TV shows, me in the conservatory brooding on the day's events. There were no ill-tempered exchanges. We barely spoke and the atmosphere was as cold as a January night.

My thinking was muddled but the focus kept coming back to the two young men we encountered coming out of Elaine's place.

I was certain that they were not – as Mandy and I had originally assumed – clients. They had threatened her, warned her off, told her to keep her mouth firmly shut on whatever it was she knew about the night Becky Walmer was murdered, and to my way of thinking, the only thing she could possibly know was the identity of the client who had secured the incriminating thread for Kitson or Penning to plant.

I was sure I had met denim jacket and jeans somewhere before, and quite recently, but as always when you're racking your brain, the answer would not come.

After such a tiring and irritating day, I was in bed for half past ten, and asleep a few minutes later. I never heard Dennis come to bed and he left for work before I got up on Thursday morning.

I still could not settle my mind, and over a sullen breakfast of muesli and half a glass of orange juice, I returned to the conservatory and waited for the phone to ring.

It would be a long wait. It was half past ten before Mandy rang and invited me to the police station to check out the footage from Huddersfield Road filling station.

Move? I was out of the house so fast that Cappy the Cat barely had time to growl a complaint at me, and I didn't spare the Diablo's horsepower as I hurried down to Haxford and into the public parking area of the station where it seemed as if everyone was waiting for me, the speed with which they hurried me through to Mandy's office.

She was in a much better frame of mind than me. She greeted me with a cheerful, "Hiya kiddo," and got straight down to business. "It was those two scroats who came out of Elaine's when we got there yesterday. Elaine's still out at The Cottage, so I've sent your Simon to pick her up."

"How's Teddy?"

"Comfortable. He wasn't too badly hurt. Broken wrist, a good few bruises, and he took a nasty knock on the head when he hit the floor. They've been watching him for signs of more serious damage, but the word is they'll probably discharge him later today." She reached for the phone. "Let me get some tea organised and we can watch the video."

I was never keen on police canteen tea, but ten minutes later, after watching the CCTV footage, I needed it.

The attack did not take place on the forecourt but in the shop, when one of the two assailants, black fleece and joggers, deliberately threw over a display of sweets. Teddy came from behind the counter and was remonstrating with him when denim jacket threw a punch. Teddy reeled but as they came in on him, he managed to kick black fleece bang on target. Clutching at his sensitive nether regions, black fleece wasn't doubled up for long. While he was getting his breath back, denim jacket waded in with a flurry of blows, Teddy went down, and as he fell, his head struck the floor. If there had been sound, I'm sure we would have heard the crack. They waded in together, kicking and punching their prone victim, and they only stopped when one of Teddy's colleagues came hurtling in from a back room. At that point, denim jacket and black fleece ran for it, and the video ended with Teddy's colleague leaning over him and dialling emergency services on his mobile phone.

Even during my years as a police office, I couldn't recall seeing such mindless and (technically) unprovoked violence. I say technically because I knew – and I guessed Mandy did too – that it was intended as a warning to Elaine.

Still shocked by what I had just witnessed, I asked, "ID?"

"Nothing. Neither of Teddy's colleagues recognised the two men, but I did, and you did too, didn't you? The moment you saw them."

"The pair who came out of Elaine's house as we got there." I could feel my brow creasing. "I couldn't put a name to either of them, but I'm sure I've met the man in the jeans and denim jacket somewhere in the last few days."

"You said so yesterday, but unless you can think who he is and where you met him, it doesn't get us any further forward. I don't know either of them and neither did your Simon."

"Elaine will know."

"True, and I'm hoping that the damage done to Teddy will prompt her to tell us who."

We didn't have too long to wait. We passed the next quarter of an hour chatting over trivia: how was Dennis (don't ask), how was Darlene (gorgeous), where was Paddy (in Huddersfield running the investigation into Penning's death) and we were in the middle of that last topic when Simon stepped in with Elaine Anguage.

Settled with a cup of tea, she looked pale, tired, angry and as we soon learned, she was unco-operative.

"We know it was those two who called on you just before we got there yesterday," Mandy said. "What we don't know is who they are."

"Join the club."

"Come on, Elaine. You know. You must know."

"In my business you don't ask for names and when you do, they usually give false ones."

That was logical enough, and it prompted me to butt in. "Did either of them call on you the night Becky Walmer was murdered?"

She actually laughed, but it was more of cynical cackle. "You call yourself a private detective? Did you get a good look at them yesterday? Tops, they were thirty years old. The night that little tramp was murdered, they'd have been no older than ten. What the hell do you think I was up to back then? A bitta child minding while giving the johns the time of their life?"

I blushed. She was (of course) perfectly right. "My bad," I excused myself.

Mandy was not prepared to let it go that easily. "Even so, you must know who sent them, Elaine."

"I don't. I told you yesterday, I was lying about Jacko that night. Now if you're gonna do me for that, gerron with it."

Mandy threw her hands in the air, a gesture of defeat, and Simon chipped in. "Elaine, you are aware that in the last couple of days, DCI Kitson and Sergeant Penning have both been murdered?"

"I'd heard."

At this point, I guessed it was my turn again. "It's only thanks to Teddy's colleagues that he's still alive, and have you checked on Wynn?"

"She was at the hospital with Teddy when he came to pick me up." She jerked a thumb at Simon as the 'he' in question.

"You're next," I persisted.

Her face paled further, and I pushed.

"You see, the way I see it is you were warned off twenty years ago on pain of what they'd do to your children. We know Jacko was innocent, we know he wasn't in Haxford when Becky was murdered. He was fitted up and the people who did that are getting desperate because they know we're getting close. They won't risk you opening your mouth. Next time they call, they'll kill you and Teddy and Wynn. It's the only way they can guarantee their own safety."

Mandy laid it on a little thicker. "And we can't offer you much in the way of protection. We're short-handed as it is."

Simon threw his cap in the ring again. "Come on, Elaine. Tell us."

She took a sip of tea and let out a long sigh. "I'll tell you what I can, but it isn't much. That night, Jacko really was down south and he got home about five in the morning. I was whining because it was Easter and we were supposed to be taking the kids to Scarborough, so he shoved me the five hundred dabs he'd made off the Fairburn job and told me to get a bus or a train. I didn't bother. Later that day, Kitson and his pal, Penning arrested Jacko. I had one or two johns the night before, and you're right about where that thread came from. It were only later when I found one of Jacko's jumpers was missing, and I reckon that's where the thread came from. Anyway, when I got back from the police station that day, there were a coupla blokes waiting for me. I thought they were punters, but I was wrong. They warned me to shut it about Jacko. They said he'd probably get off with it when it got to court. If I didn't keep my trap shut, I wouldn't see my kids again." Elaine shrugged and drank more tea. "What could I do? The filth, that slime Kitson and Penning told Jacko the same thing and that's why he coughed to killing her. At that stage, neither of us knew they had that thread from under that lass's fingernail. Then when it came to court, Jacko got life and I kicked off. I had another visit from them but I told them this time that if I didn't shout about it, it'd look suspicious. They could deal with that as long as I didn't say too much. And that's how it was until you came poking your nose in."

On those last words, she pointed an accusing finger at me.

I could only shrug. "Sorry, Elaine, but I was prompted. Someone fed me the bottom line on Del Tyndall's confession."

"Let's not get distracted," Mandy said before focussing on Elaine. "What happened yesterday?"

"I tell you, I don't know who they were, but

they called to ram home the message. I told 'em to sod off, and I reckon that's when they decided to show me they meant it and they went after Teddy."

"But you don't know them?" Mandy insisted.

"Didn't I just say so?"

"What about the two men all those years ago?" I asked. "Did you know either of them?"

"Not at the time."

Mandy leapt upon the information. "But you do now?"

"One of 'em turned into a regular. I don't know his proper name, but he likes to be known as Doggy cos he likes—"

Given her trade, I could see where she was going and I cut her off. "Yes, Elaine. I think we get the picture."

She scowled. "I was gonna say he likes his greyhounds. He has two or three, and he used to race 'em at one time. Anyway, like I said, he became a regular. Big, he was." She glared at me. "And I don't mean what you think I mean. I mean he was tall, all muscle and strong as an ox."

"But you don't know his real name?"

"I told you I didn't. What is it with you people? Do you not listen? I haven't seen him in a long while, and I figured he was keeping an eye on me as much as getting his jollies."

"And you can't tell us anymore about him?" Mandy demanded.

"Not really. From the clobber he used to wear, I guessed he was builder, but I can't tell you nowt other than that."

An alert rang through my head. Builder,

Springer's Building Supplies. Argument between Brian Springer and overall and rigger boots. How could I describe him? I didn't have to. I videoed it from outside Springer's office.

While Mandy and Elaine continued playing verbal ping-pong, I accessed the video on my smartphone scrolled it to the correct place and paused it. I set it on the table and turned it to face Elaine. "Is that Doggy?"

She took her time. She even hit the 'play' icon to watch the video and at one point, I saw her features change imperceptibly. It was almost too quick to notice, but I spotted it as recognition.

Eventually, she passed the phone back to me. "That's him. Older'n I remember him, but it's definitely Doggy."

Mandy and I exchanged what I called 'the glance' it was an unspoken agreement that we both knew what had to happen next.

Elaine hastened on. "It wasn't him who called yesterday, and he didn't smack our Teddy about. Crikey, must be ten years since I seen Doggy."

"We're aware that it wasn't him yesterday," Mandy said. "Even so, you've already admitted that he threatened you twenty years ago. There's no statute of limitations in this country."

Elaine's features clouded. "Statue of what?"

"It means he can still be prosecuted," I explained.

"Waste of time if you ask me. He's only gonna deny it, and the kids never saw him."

"Leave that to us." Mandy made a few notes on her pad. "That's it, Elaine. That's all we need.

189

Thanks for your help. Simon, can you run her back to The Cottage?"

"And then what, Sarge?"

"By the time you get back, me and your mam should have a proper ID on this guy, and we'll get a team together to bring him in."

Simon nodded. "Make sure you pencil my name at the top of the team sheet."

They left and Mandy turned to me. "Where and when did you get that video?"

"Springer's Building Supplies the day you and I met at Terry's. The day I received Jephcott's video. They were arguing, Mandy. Springer and this Doggy character. Right after I'd spoke to Springer and the Farmer woman, Springer's PA. The video was a spur of the moment thing, and haven't you been saying that whoever had Penning and Kitson killed is spending a lot of money to shut people up. Brian Springer is worth a lot of money, and he had a track record for womanising. Linda Risley told me that if Springer hadn't tried his luck with Becky, she'd be very surprised. And remember the lie about his wife being with him? Suppose that on the night, he wasn't with Nancy Farmer but tried it on with Becky, she told him where to go, and he followed her home."

"And yet, during the original investigation, Pauline Springer told us he was with her all night."

"It's called lying, Mandy. As a long-serving cop, you should know all about it."

She stood. "No evidence, though, so let's concentrate on this Doggy guy. Elaine might not know who he is, but Brian Springer will."

Chapter Seventeen

"You took a video of me talking to one of my customers? I'm sure that must be an invasion of privacy."

In the past, Mandy's presence would bolster my confidence when faced with Brian Springer's outrage, but these days, largely thanks to my work for Radio Haxford, I found it didn't matter. I would be just as calm and in control if I were alone.

"Frankly, Mr Springer, I didn't trust you," I told him. "And I didn't see you talking, I saw you arguing with this man. So soon after our discussion re Becky Walmer, I thought the two circumstances might be linked. And all Sergeant Hiscoe needs is his name."

He was seriously affronted, and it showed. "Do you know who you're dealing with?"

At that point, Mandy took over. "This is a murder inquiry, sir, and if necessary I'll apply for a court order requiring you to divulge his name. I'm trying to short circuit that to ensure no one else is hurt. The alternative is, I haul you to the station where you'll likely face charges of obstruction and withholding information."

This time it was shock. "You can't do that."

Mandy was more than equal to the challenge.

"Try me."

Springer reached for the phone. "I'm calling my solicitor."

"Fine. Tell him to come to the police station." Mandy stood up. "Brian Springer, I'm arresting you for obstructing the police in the course of their inquiries and withholding information relevant to an ongoing investigation. I must caution you—"

"Wait, wait, wait." Springer dropped the phone and Mandy sat down again.

We've all heard the term pregnant pause but there was nothing pregnant about that which followed, or if there was, it came to term pretty quickly.

"Callum Denby." Springer delivered the name with an air of resignation, as if it was the last thing he wanted to do. If my growing suspicions were correct, it probably was the last thing he wanted to do, because Callum Denby would be able to point the finger... at Brian Springer or his wife, except that I knew it couldn't be his wife.

Mandy stood and I joined her. As we reached the door, Springer spoke again.

"You should be careful. Denby is a big, strong man, and he's quick-tempered when he's crossed. He'll tear the two of you apart."

Mandy smiled. "Thanks for the warning, Mr Springer, but I have plenty of people I can call on, and it doesn't matter how tough he is, Denby won't take them all."

As we made our way out to Mandy's car, I said, "We have him to find, and I'll bet Springer is on the phone to him right now. By the time we track him down, he'll have disappeared."

She took out her phone. "Which is why you and I are going back to the station. I'll get the team after him now."

We climbed into her car while she was speaking to the station, and once we were settled, she ended the called.

"Sorted," she reported.

(Did you see what I did there? Sorted and reported. Not only a radio star, but a poet, too.)

"Your Simon is leading the team and they know exactly where to find Denby. He's on that conversion job out at Christmas Manor, but he should be on his way to the station by the time we get back there."

We were parked facing away from Springer's office but Mandy checked her mirror as she started the engine. "You were right. He's on the horn, probably to Denby. Won't make any difference. There's only the one road to and from Christmas Manor. You suspect him don't you? Springer, I mean."

I nodded. "He was always an outside bet, but Linda confirmed that he was a bed-hopper, and my guess is he tried it with Becky and she kicked him back. So he went after her later that night. Maybe he didn't mean to kill her—"

Mandy interrupted. "No way. If some guy wrapped his hands round her throat, fine, I'd take manslaughter, but he used a ligature. He meant to shut her up. So maybe he did have his way with Becky and she was piling the pressure on for a promotion or pay rise or something. But don't forget his missus. If she knew, maybe she decided to deal with the problem in her own way."

Now I shook my head. "She was in the maternity ward at The Cottage. Remember?"

Accelerating along Sheffield Road, Mandy chuckled. "An outside bet, did you say? I'd say the odds are shortening."

"It's all circumstantial, Mandy. You'll need a confession."

"Leave it to me… when we're through with Denby."

She was right about one thing. When we got to the station we were greeted with the news that it took several constables to subdue and handcuff Denby, but he was in the back of a patrol car and on his way there.

But it wasn't all plain sailing when he arrived. He was furious and demanded a solicitor. That, Mandy told me, would take the better part of an hour, maybe longer, and in any event, they had to wait for Paddy to get there from Huddersfield.

"Not much point me hanging around," I said, and it was then that I noticed Simon sporting a black eye. "Have you been fighting, or did you criticise Naomi's cooking?"

"Denby," he told me. "Come on, Mam, let's go get a cuppa. I need a word or three."

This was a puzzle and it sent a buzz of alarm through me as I followed Simon up the stairs to the canteen. "Nothing wrong with Bethany, is there?"

"No. Beth's fine. It's Dad."

An even bigger puzzle, although I felt it might help clear up the mystery of what was ailing Dennis.

He was guaranteed to be more open with Simon than he would be with me for two reasons. One, he would not want me to worry, and two, he wouldn't suffer the same backlash from Simon as he might from me, especially if he'd done something he shouldn't have.

Simon pointed me to a table over by the windows, from where we could look out on the traffic of the northern by-pass, while he went to the counter and returned a few minutes later with two cups of tea.

After the aggravation I'd endured over the last week or more, I was in no mood for prevarication, and I got straight to the point. "So what's wrong with your father?"

"Nothing. In fact, that's exactly the same question he asked me, but he wanted to know what was wrong with you."

"Well—"

"Take last Saturday, f'rinstance. I didn't know why Paddy Quinn wanted you but he asked me to track you down. According to Dad, you went ballistic when you found out he'd told me where you were."

"I'd just been arrested, love."

"I know that, but it wasn't without cause, was it? You broke the law, Mam, and you of all people should know there's a price to pay for that."

"Your father and I have put it right since."

"Not according to Dad, you haven't. He says you're spending every night in the conservatory, on your own instead of with him in the front room."

"Because I'm not interested in repeats of Top

195

Gear or Bangers & Cash. I wasn't interested in them first time round." I decided it was time to come off the defensive. "There is something wrong, Simon, but I think it's with your father, not me, and he won't say what it is."

"Let me have a word with him. If that's right, he'll tell me. To be fair, Mam, me and Naomi have noticed a change in you. You're more... I don't know... aggressive. That's probably not the right word. You're certainly ready to challenge anyone and everyone, and that's not my mam. You met those bods in Cambridge head on especially that DCI Rothman, and according to Mandy, you've been championing Prater's case from the word go."

"And I've been proven right, haven't I? I'm not about to apologise for that, love."

"And I don't say you should. I'm just commenting on the change that's come over you." He checked his watch. "I'd better get back down to the interview room or Mandy'll be kicking off. I'll catch you later, and hey, have a word with the old man. I don't like to see my folks falling out."

I gave him a mother's peck on the cheek and he left me alone; alone and wondering whether he was right. Had I changed that much? Was that what Dennis had been trying to tell me for the last week or two?

After thirty years, there was not much I didn't know about my other half. When it came to practical work he had no equal, but he was not good with words. It was why he tended to bluntness. It was easier for him to say what was on his mind and hang the consequences than try to work out a diplomatic means of getting the message across. But such outspokenness with me would invariably lead to an argument, and it occurred to me that perhaps he had been trying to avoid that clash. If so, he hadn't succeeded.

Sitting there, thinking about it, two comments leapt into my mind, and both came from me. Arrested, faced with Paddy and Mandy, I had shouted, *I'm Christine Capper. Remember? Ex-cop and a radio star. I have influence.* A few days later, at Huddersfield police station, confronted with Nocton and Bentil, I insisted, *I'm Christine Capper. Ex-cop, private eye, blogger, vlogger and a radio star.* I also recalled that on both occasions, I asked myself if I'd really said that.

Simon (and Dennis) may have had a point, I decided, but right now, I had more to worry about; like the interview between the police and Callum Denby.

With hindsight, I would query my priorities, but at the time, the Prater case, the murder of Becky Walmer, and my determination to crack both, were as much to blame for my new found assertiveness and (unproven) change in character as anything.

Because it was an official, police interview, the only people allowed in the room were police officers and the suspect's solicitor, but after Mandy persuaded him, Paddy graciously allowed me to watch from the observation room with Fliss Keele sat alongside me (to ensure I didn't get out of my pram, I suppose).

From the outset, Denby, a much larger and more intimidating man than I remembered from my first visit to Springer's, took his solicitor's advice and refused to say anything more than 'no comment' to every question.

I estimated his height at something like six feet six. Broad shouldered, there wasn't a trace of fat on him, and I guessed that if he stripped off his shirt, his upper body would be packed with muscle. His weatherbeaten face was half obscured by a rough beard, but despite his repeated, 'no comment' his eyes were pinpoints of fury.

Everything changed when Mandy challenged him with our prior knowledge. "We have testimony from Elaine Anguage that you, Mr Denby, threatened her on the night after Rebecca Walmer's murder. You not only threatened Elaine but her children, too. She says that you told her to keep her mouth shut about Jack Prater's non-involvement in that crime."

Denby rose, his fists clenched, ready to strike out.

Paddy Quinn was tall, fit, and knew how to look after himself, but he wasn't stupid. He had two male constables in the room, and as Denby stood, they moved in, ready to subdue him.

"Sit down, Mr Denby," Paddy ordered. "You're in enough trouble as it is. Don't make it worse for yourself."

His solicitor, too, urged Denby to calm down, and he gradually acquiesced.

Paddy took the lead. "Now, how do you answer Elaine Anguage's claim?"

"All right, all right. So me and a pal went along there and told her to shut it, but we were only larking around. Someone shoved us a couple of hundred notes to do it. We didn't know what it was about. Anyway, she made enough money off me afterwards. I was calling on her once a week for a bit of horizontal, and she didn't do it for free. Know what I mean?"

Mandy shifted the subject sideways. "Last night, Elaine's son, Teddy, was assaulted at the petrol station where he works. This was after Elaine herself was threatened. Were you underlining your message of twenty years ago, Denby?"

He almost lost it again. "That was nothing to do with me. You want to know about that, talk to Springer's lad, Robbie. I'm not carrying the can for something he did."

This was news to me. I knew the Springers had a daughter. She was born in the days before Becky was murdered, but no one had mentioned a son.

At that point, Paddy suspended the interview, promised to send in the refreshments for Denby and his solicitor, and he and Mandy came out of the interview room. I met them on the corridor where Paddy was giving Simon instructions.

"Take a couple of uniforms and get down to Springer's yard. If he's there, bring Robbie Springer in."

"Excuse me, Paddy," I butted in. "Would you mind if I accompanied Simon?"

"Yes, I would. This is getting dirtier, Christine, and I don't want you at risk."

"Very well. I'll follow them."

"Christine—"

I cut him off. "Letter of the law, Paddy. You

199

can't stop me." And with that, I left the station, climbed into the Diablo, and fired up the engine, ready to follow my son.

Simon didn't appear to be in a hurry. I let down the window as he approached the car.

"This could be dangerous, Mam. I don't want you anywhere near it."

"You're forgetting, Simon. I started all this. I'm not going to interfere with your work, but it may be that I can identify this man. When we get there, I'll wait in the car."

He shook his head. "Dad's right, Mother. You're becoming impossible."

That was a bad sign. Simon only ever called me 'mother' when he was annoyed with me.

To my surprise, it was pushing up half past four when we pulled out of the station car park into the increasing, rush-hour traffic, and it took as the better part of twenty-five minutes to get to Springer's yard on Sheffield Road, and I did as I promised, and stayed in the car while Simon and the two uniforms went into the building.

They came out again a few minutes later, and Simon came to me. "He's not here, and Springer doesn't know where he is."

"You need to get onto Paddy, tell him to watch Elaine Anguage's place, and get someone out to The Cottage, in case he's hanging around there waiting for Teddy to be discharged." I put my brain into gear trying to think of anywhere else Springer the younger might be. "Wynn works at CutCost, so he might have gone there to watch for her. I can't think of…" I trailed off as a shock run through me. "Oh

200

my God. Haxford Mill. Your father was threatened."

Simon shook his head. "At this time, Grimy, Geronimo, and Greg Vetch will still be there with him."

"Yes, but they could be watching, waiting for Tony, Lester, and Greg going home."

Simon nodded. "I'll get onto it."

Right at that moment, my phone rang. I checked the screen, and read 'Hazel McQuarrie'. I made the connection. "Hazel? What's wrong, love?"

"You'd better get home, Chrissy. A pair of hooligans have just thrown a brick through your front window."

Chapter Eighteen

I was ready for tearing off home, but Simon stayed me, rang the station to bring them up to speed, and then instructed me to follow him.

He took the wheel of the patrol car, and in direct contravention of all the rules, switched on the headlights and blue, emergency lights, and roared off out of Springer's yard with me clinging to his tail.

I knew who it was. Robbie Springer and his pal. It had to be them. They had threatened Elaine, picked up Teddy, and now they were turning their attention upon me. It was a good thing that I wasn't home, or I could have ended up in The Cottage alongside Teddy Anguage.

Curiously enough, as we tore up the hill towards Bracken Close, my concern was for Cappy the Cat. Moody, sullen, sulky, greedy, and lazy, he might be, but he was my cat, my pet, and if they had harmed him...

I shut the thought off before it could fully materialise.

With traffic getting out of the way of a police car on an emergency, we pulled up outside the drive ten minutes after leaving Springer's, and even from the driver's seat of the Diablo, the damage was appalling.

The front window was a large, picture window, with two side lights. The centre pane was missing. And it was a sealed unit. I guessed that they must have thrown the brick (or whatever missile had done the damage) twice. Once to deal with the outer pane, the second time to get rid of the inner. I didn't know how much it would cost, but I doubted that we would get much change out of £2000. Naturally, we had insurance, but without checking the small print of the policies, I didn't know whether it would cover criminal damage. Whether it did or not, I vowed I would see the Springer family, or certainly the two men, in court.

The damage inside the house was minimal, and it was obvious that they had not climbed through the missing window. Sonny Scott told us as much after speaking to both Hazel McQuarrie and Fred and Barbara Timmins, our immediate neighbours. When the outer pane smashed, Fred and Barbara came out to see what was going on, and when the inner pane went, Hazel appeared at her door. At that point, the attackers climbed into an ageing Toyota, and fled.

There was a house brick on the carpet, a note Sellotaped to it, and it was surrounded by shattered glass. I only hoped that the Dyson could suck it all up without doing any damage to the machine's internal gubbins. Suck up the glass, I mean, not the brick. That machine was brilliant but I don't think it could cope with something that big and heavy.

Mercifully, Cappy the Cat was all right. We found him sleeping in his basket (what else was new) and when I checked him over, I found some small cuts to his paw. He'd obviously trodden on some of the broken glass, presumably making his way to find out what was going on in the hope that whoever threw the brick might also throw him some food.

I went to pick up the brick, but Simon stopped me. "Don't touch it, Mam. With a bit of luck, these dorks might have left us some dabs."

He pulled on a pair of forensic gloves, picked up the brick, and gently peeled the note away. He unfolded it as a single sheet of A4 paper, and read the message.

His features darkened as he passed it to me.

You hasn't listened you stupid bag.

I tutted. "Idiots can't even write plain English." And then I realised. "Dennis. They'll go after Dennis." I dragged out my phone and with a shaking hand, rang him.

"What you want, woman? Don't you understand the word busy?"

"Shut up, Dennis, and listen. Someone has just taken out our front window, and left a note. It's a threat, and I'm certain they're coming for you."

"Smashed the window? Do you know how much that'll cost?"

"Are you listening to me, Dennis? They're coming after you."

He wasn't listening. "That'll set us back two and a half grand. When are you gonna learn to mind your own business?"

I was practically screaming into the phone. "You are in danger, you idiot. Get in your car and come home now."

"I don't have time for this rubbish. I've told you before, I'm all right. Now can I get on?"

Simon took the phone from me. "Dad, it's Simon. I was with Mam when she got the phone call telling her about the window, and she's right. It looks like they're coming for you. If she'd been home, they might have had a go at her, but she was with us. Now, for crying out loud, do as Mam says, and get the hell out of there."

I couldn't hear what Dennis said, but a moment later, the phone bleeped to indicate that the connection was terminated. My son glared at it for a moment, and handed it back to me.

"Sorry, Mam, he wouldn't listen."

I was on the verge of panic. "I'll have to get down there."

"No you don't." Simon turned to Sonny Scott. "Hold the fort here, Sonny. Check the garage, see if you can find wooden planks, or something, to cover the window. I'll take the car and get Mam down to Haxford Mill to make sure the old man's all right."

As we prepared to leave, I advised Sonny, "if Cappy the Cat gives you any trouble, you'll find food for him in one of the kitchen cupboards. Just put a feed down and he'll be all right."

And with that, Simon and I hurried out to the patrol car.

Once again, he put the headlights and flashing, blue lights on, turned the car round, and sped out of Bracken Close, down the hill towards Haxford centre, his siren screaming when traffic got in the way. And as he drove, he called into the station, and brought them up to speed on the gathering momentum of events.

It was quarter to six when we hurtled into Haxford Mill yard, and slurred to a halt outside Haxford Fixers' premises. I couldn't see Tony Wharrier's car, nor Greg Vetch's, and Lester Grimes didn't drive, so it wasn't an option. But right away, I spotted an old Toyota parked alongside the canal wall, and my fears reached a peak.

"Oh, no. They're already here."

Simon was out of the car faster than me, and I was moving quickly. We rushed into the workshop and stopped dead. Denim jacket and black fleece were seated on uncomfortable chairs, bound into place with what looked like thin, metal wire, wrapped many times round their hands and wrists and across their chests. Both had a number of bruises about their faces.

In the background, Dennis, Tony, Lester, and Greg were talking softly amongst each other.

"What's going on?" I asked.

Dennis grinned. "After you rang, Geronimo, Grimy, and Herriot made it look like they were leaving for the night."

"Greg and I moved our cars one at a time round the corner out of sight," Tony Wharrier explained.

Greg Vetch delivered the next line. "But in fact, it was Tony who moved them all. The rest of us were still in here."

"And these idiots didn't realise?" I asked, pointing at the two offenders.

"I just wore a different coat each time," Tony said.

"And then I made like I was going for me bus,"

Lester chuckled.

"And when they came in, they met three of us, with Geronimo behind, stopping them getting away," Dennis explained. He spoke next to Simon. "We had to slap 'em about a bit, lad."

"No worries, Dad. Self-defence and reasonable restraint, I reckon."

Lester gave me a salacious grin. "And we did it all for you, Chrissy. Don't you think I deserve a wild night with you after that?"

"I'll bear it in mind, thank you, Lester." I concentrated on Dennis. "You told me I was talking rubbish."

"Aye, I did, but I heard you wittering on about Teddy Anguage last night, so we sorted it out. We were ready for 'em, Chrissy." He looked to Simon. "There you are, our lad. They're all yours."

Simon got straight on the phone to the station, calling for reinforcements to take the two offenders away, and while we waited, I glowered at denim jacket.

"Your father is going to pay for the damage you did, young Springer."

He tried to sneer, but the bruises obviously hurt, and instead he winced. "I don't know what you're talking about."

"We have you on video all over the place," Simon told him. "You are looking at a comfortable two to three years in the nick for the damage you did to my mother's house, and for the damage you did to Teddy Anguage yesterday, and for threatening Elaine Anguage yesterday. And if you topped Frank Penning or Pete Kitson, you'll be looking at life."

"No comment."

Simon ignored the blatant goad, and spoke to Dennis. "We have two cars on the way here, Dad. The minute we get these scroats away, take Mam home, and you'd better call someone out to do a proper job on the front window."

Dennis pointed an angry finger at denim jacket, practically certain to be Robbie Springer. "Can we make these clowns pay for the window?" Typical Dennis. Simon's instruction reminded him of the money it would cost rather than concentrating on our safety.

"Leave that to me, Dennis," I said. "We might have to pay out up front, but we will get that money back, probably off our insurance company, or if not, then through the courts when we sue him or his father. Simon's right. The front room's a heck of a mess. Broken glass everywhere. We need to get it cleaned up, and like Simon says, we need to get someone to do a proper job on that front window, board it up until we can get it replaced."

It wasn't entirely a surprise when Greg Vetch spoke up. "You don't need to call anyone, Chrissy." He turned to Dennis. "Do you have any sheets of MDF or hardboard, or something, Cappy?"

"Plenya stuff kicking about in the garage."

"I'll come with you, and I can deal with the front window while you and Chrissy clean up inside."

Tony also volunteered. "If you need any assistance, Val and I are not doing anything this evening."

Not to be left out, Lester chipped in. "I can give you an hour, but after that... Well, you know how I'm fixed."

Dennis scowled. "Yeah. The Sump Hole'll be open then."

Lester grinned. "Got it in one, Cappy."

I felt a sudden burst of love for these men. I'd known Tony and Lester for years, I'd known Greg for just about one year, but Dennis and I couldn't wish for more supportive friends. "You're very kind. All of you. And if you really don't mind helping, I'll make sure we at least feed you."

"I'd rather have the cash," Lester said, but everyone shouted him down.

As it turned out, Lester would be there for a lot longer than an hour.

It was a monumental task. Not so much taking down the boards Sonny Scott had put in place, or for Dennis, Greg, and Lester putting up proper replacements, but for Tony and me cleaning the carpet and furniture of every trace of glass.

Cappy the Cat was not best pleased. He was quite used to a houseful of people and accustomed to ignoring them when they refused to feed him, but he did not enjoy being thrown out of his basket and the front room, while I checked said basket for glass, and then set it down in the conservatory. I also noticed that he was limping on his right, front paw. I checked the paw (despite his protests) with a magnifying glass but I couldn't see anything, and that would entail a visit to the vet on Friday morning. Not one of Cappy the Cat's favourite ports of call, and considering his habit of lashing out at anyone who dared to examine him, I don't think Cappy the Cat was too popular with the vet.

Luckily, at the time of year (early May in case you weren't paying attention) it stayed light until gone nine o'clock, and we were finished by half past eight, at which time I insisted all four of them sit at the kitchen table while I served beers and thawed a quartet of frozen dinners. I had enough to do getting all the glass up from the carpet, so there was no way I'd start cooking a proper meal for four from scratch, and anyway, no one complained. They were too busy feeding themselves and taking pity on a limping Cappy the Cat by throwing him scraps. Dumb animals? Cappy the Cat was so dumb he knew how to play on peoples' sympathy.

There was a distinct work atmosphere in the kitchen. They talked about cars, engines, torque (which I thought they did enough of because I misread 'torque' as 'talk' and they were talking all the time) power to weight ratios and so on, none of which made any sense to me. Tony chipped in with bodywork observations, and Lester managed a word now and then on electrical issues associated with modern cars. It was as if they'd never left the workshop. And throughout it all, there wasn't a single mention of the coronation. Was I the only person in Haxford who was looking forward to it?

Meanwhile, I waited on them like a good hostess, clearing away the detritus of their main meal and treating them to apple pie (defrosted) and whipped cream (from a tube) for afters. Well, it was better than being totally left out.

They left before ten o'clock, at which time

Dennis and I set about tidying up. That took us up to almost half past and by then I was exhausted. I had intended to bring up the chat between Simon and me, but Dennis was in a mood over the probable cost of the new window and I was so tired that I knew it would lead to an argument, so I took myself off to bed. I didn't even have time to finish my bedtime cup of tea before I was asleep.

Chapter Nineteen

Friday morning dawned sunny and bright, but with a chilly wind blowing in from the moors. Annoying. We were used to rising temperatures at this time of year, and I did like to make a start on the garden in early May. When I commented on this to Dennis over breakfast he was busy feeding himself so all I got was a non-committal grunt.

Cappy the Cat was still limping, so the first task of the day was getting him into the pet carrier (difficult) and to the vet's surgery on Stone Street, just off the southern town centre bypass (easy) where, after struggling with our malicious moggie, and examining the offending paw through a better magnifying glass than mine, the vet announced that there were one or two tiny cuts. He removed some tiny shards of glass, prescribed some ointment, put Cappy the Cat in a cone of shame to stop him licking the ointment off, and charged me thirty pounds for the privilege.

Driving back home, I came to the conclusion that I was in the wrong job. True, as a private eye I charged more than thirty pounds an hour, but the vet secured the same amount for less than ten minutes work and a few claw marks on the back of his hand. For once, I almost approved of Cappy the Cat's fightback. Indeed, I would have applauded it had the little swine not already clawed the back of my hand when I was pushing him into the pet carrier.

When I got him home, I had to help him out of the thing because the cone kept getting in the way, and once he was out, he limped a few paces, then turned and glared up at me as if asking, 'Why have you fitted me with a satellite dish?' He disappeared to the front room and his basket, but we'd moved it because of the broken glass, so he was back inside a minute, hobbling his way to the conservatory with a face that said, 'You, woman, are taxing my patience.'

Second breakfast (coffee and a chocolate digestive) called and as I sat munching, my thoughts naturally turned to the Prater case.

A quick call to Mandy told me that they hadn't yet started the interrogation of Robbie Springer and his pal. It was too late the previous afternoon and they were waiting for solicitors. It was no more than an assumption that denim jacket was Robbie Springer. Both suspects had refused to give their names and addresses (an offence in itself). They also rejected the notion of calling Brian Springer, and it was easy to see why. It would give the game away.

Beyond that, Mandy had nothing to tell me, and I could do nothing other than cast my mind back over the week and then some since the video first landed in my inbox.

Elaine Anguage's words rang round my head. I called myself a private detective? To press I had made precious little progress. All right, so I had all but proved that Jack Prater was innocent, but when it came to the murder of Becky Walmer, I was no further forward than on day one.

I had narrowed down the suspects to one person. Brian Springer. It had to be him. He lied to me when he said he was with his wife at Jumping Jacks that night. She was in maternity with her new daughter. He had enough money to buy off Kitson and Penning, he had more than enough to arrange Kitson's demise, and his son and accomplice had dealt with Frank Penning, and later hammered Teddy Anguage. Not only that, but he knew Denby, the same thug who had threatened Elaine Anguage. Everything pointed to Brian Springer, but it was all circumstantial and it would be thrown out of court… if it ever got there. I had not one shred of hard evidence let alone proof.

It was almost as if Mandy could read my mind. I was thinking of Denby and she rang back.

"I forgot to tell you that we've charged Denby with threatening behaviour. We held him overnight and he's up before the beak this morning. It's years since he pressured Elaine, and as you know, he thought it as just a bit of a lark."

"And of course, he's been a little angel since, hasn't he?"

"Deffo. Well, put it this way, we've had nothing on him since. Self-employed, reputable builder, kind to his employees, always pays his taxes on the dot. He'll probably get a suspended sentence or community service or something."

"I wonder if Jack Prater will see it that way when he's finally released."

Negative as it was, Mandy's call automatically turned my attention to the video which had identified Denby, and as much for want of something to do, something to occupy my mind, I ran it.

Springer certainly looked very aeriated and all Denby could do was stand there shrugging his massive shoulders. It didn't look as if he managed to say anything. Mind you, it would have been difficult. Springer didn't shut up long enough for Denby to get a word in.

To add an air of innocence to the video, I'd panned round the yard as well as focussing on Springer's office and as I did so, I spotted brown stockman's coat with his clipboard, and I recalled thinking at the time that the argument in Springer's office could well have something to do with Denby having a grievance. He had, after all, been wandering round the yard with brown stockman's coat.

Nothing Denby had said would dispute that, but...

My thoughts came to a stuttering halt. Brown stockman's coat. It was him. Denim jacket and jeans. The man Dennis and his partners had trapped. He worked for Springer. If he wasn't Springer's son, then they would know who he was, and whatever the relationship, it strengthened my belief that Brian Springer was behind everything that had happened.

I rang Mandy, but was told that she was unavailable. The solicitor(s) must have turned up and she would be interviewing the pair. Either that or she was in court to give evidence against Denby.

I left a message for her, then flew out of the house, jumped into the Diablo and made for Springer's.

I did not anticipate a cheerful welcome and Springer didn't let me down. He must have seen me from his office because as I hurried into reception, he was there.

"Get out, Mrs Capper. Now. I don't want to see you here again."

"For your information, Mr Springer, I'm working with the police and they're busy right now… interrogating your son and his mate who murdered Frank Penning, and were in the process of trying to kill Teddy Anguage when they were disturbed. They then targeted my husband, but they came unstuck. Dennis and his pals had them tied up with wire when the cops got there."

"I don't know what or who you're talking about. Now for the second and last time, get out."

I stood my ground and held up my phone. "I have him on video. The one I took of you and Denby arguing. And the cops have him on CCTV footage from both the petrol station on Huddersfield Road and my husband's place. And if I'm right, it won't be long before they come for you… for strangling Becky Walmer."

Oh dear. That was a mouthful too far for Springer. He came at me, fists clenched and for one brief second, I thought it would be lights out.

"Mr Springer," I heard Nancy Farmer scream. "Brian. No."

It must have clicked in his brain because instead of lashing out at me, he grabbed me by the coat, opened the door and bundled me out so roughly that I ended up on the ground.

"And don't come back," he shouted.

Embarrassed? Everyone in the yard was looking at me, but no one came to my assistance. I could feel my cheeks burning but I persuaded myself that it was anger. Who did he think he was? He couldn't treat me like that. I was Christine Capper. Private eye, vlogger, radio star… there it was again. I was no longer a radio star. I'd been fired.

Mustering as much aplomb as I could gather, which involved ignoring the amazed stares coming my way, I got to my feet and went back to my car, and in an act of sheer defiance, while Springer looked on from his office window, I rang the police station, demanded to speak to either Mandy or Paddy, and eventually got the inspector.

It didn't often happen that Paddy would listen to me, but he did now, and when I was through explaining the situation, he said, "You're not a cop and he wasn't obliged to speak to you, Chrissy, so you should have come to us. It's too late to worry about that now. Stay there. I'm on my way."

Satisfied, I jammed a CD of Orchestral Manoeuvres in the Dark into the car's player, and settled back to try and calm down. It didn't work and not because of OMD, but thanks to Brian Springer.

He must have watched me for the better part of five minutes before he came storming from the building, across the car park, and yanked open my door.

"Are you just stupid or don't you understand

plain English. Get yourself and this heap of crap off my premises."

"I can't."

"Then I'll get a gang to push you out into the street."

"The police are on their way and I've been ordered to stay here."

"For the last time... What? What did you say?"

"You heard. DI Quinn is on his way and he's ordered me to stay where I am. And when he gets here, he's going to be demanding some explanations from you regarding your son's activities. You know who I mean. The son you refused to identify, the son who's under arrest at Haxford police station, the son who's going to prison for murder and attempted murder. And I know Paddy Quinn. When he bites, your little Robbie will be only too keen to tell the police who paid him to kill Frank Penning, then attack Teddy Anguage and my husband. You're sunk, Mr Springer, you and your rotten family."

I thought he would stomp off back to his office. I was wrong. He grabbed at my coat, ready to drag me out of the car. Scared? More frightened and I'd have to go home and put clean knickers on.

I yanked the key from the ignition. The sound of OMD cut out right away, and was replaced by the sound of Brian Springer howling when I jabbed the point of the ignition key into the soft part of his hand, that fold of skin between thumb and forefinger. It wasn't sharp but it was enough to make him back off.

Satisfied with his reaction and retreat, I said, "Go back to your office. I'll be here until the police arrive." With that, I closed the door and hit the dashboard switch to lock the car up all round.

That would teach him to mess with Christine Capper.

If I'd stopped to think about it, I'd be amazed at the number of times I could get it wrong in so short a period.

Springer did not go back to his office. Instead, he crossed the yard to a stack of loose bricks, took one, came back to the car, and threw it at the windscreen. It cracked. The windscreen, I mean, not the brick.

I was already cowering because I expected it to shatter and shower me with glass. I had an instant and idiotic vision of me at the vet's where they put me in a cone of shame, and Cappy the Cat gloating over my predicament and saying, 'Instant karma. See how you like it.'

Dennis was the real expert on windscreens and he always insisted on laminated, not toughened, even though they were more expensive. Aside from the price, what's the difference? No point asking me, but perhaps that was why the screen only cracked rather than shattering.

Not to be beaten by the pedantry of a humble motor mechanic, Springer picked the brick up and instead of throwing it, began to beat the windscreen. When that wouldn't yield, he turned his attention to the driver's window. Laminated glass? Toughened glass? Reconstituted brandy glass? I didn't know, but I do know that unlike the screen, it fractured into a million pieces and on the second blow, it gave way and I was covered in fragments.

Cone of shame, here I come, I thought.

Springer had other ideas. He reached in, his hands groping for my throat. I jabbed the key time and again into his skin, but he wasn't for letting go again. Another idea occurred to him. He backed off, picked up the brick and aimed at my head.

I screamed, ducked my head over to the passenger seat and covered it with my hands. I was consumed with terror and I guessed I would be on my way to either A&E or the mortuary in the next few minutes. I prayed for the former.

In such a dire situation, it's odd the things that rush through your mind. The main thing was why didn't I listen to Dennis? Because he never talked about anything other than cars was why. But he didn't just talk about cars. He made occasional observations, usually along the lines of, why did I insist on poking my nose in where it didn't concern me?

At that moment, shaking in utter terror, convinced that I was as close to the end as I wanted to be for a woman my age, waiting for the brick to strike and catapult me into oblivion, I wished I had never heard of Becky Walmer and Jack Prater. I wished Ivan Jephcott had picked on another private eye (difficult considering there weren't any in Haxford). I wished I'd taken Paddy's advice and left it to the police. I thought of Bethany, the hyperactive little girl who I would never see grow up. I thought of Simon, always keen to make his mum so proud of him, of Naomi, the daughter-in-law who became the daughter I always wanted, of Ingrid, the daughter I had, a woman as determined and single-minded as her mother, of Dennis, an awkward so-and-so when he wanted, but the husband who had been there for the last thirty years, a rock, a constant in our lives of ups and downs.

The brick never came. Help did, and it came from an unexpected quarter.

I heard a lot of shouting, I heard Springer ranting loud enough to be heard in Huddersfield. I heard the click of the driver's door manual release as someone reached in through the shattered window and opened said door.

"Are you all right, Mrs Capper?"

I recognised the voice of Nancy Farmer, and cautiously sat up.

A group of people, a mix of staff and customers, were holding Brian Springer back, he was screaming into the sky and using some pretty choice language, which I wouldn't repeat.

"Are you okay, Mrs Capper?"

Nancy's repeated query barely registered. I broke down and wept.

Chapter Twenty

Paddy, Simon, and a brace of uniforms turned up a few minute later, by which time I'd calmed down, helped by a cup of tea from Nancy Farmer.

When told what had happened, Simon was all out for giving Springer a taste of his own medicine, but Paddy called him to order and I backed the inspector's words.

"He's not worth the trouble it'll cause for you, love."

Paddy picked up on that, but his comment was aimed at me. "And it's not worth the trouble you're getting yourself into, Chrissy. Just back off. You've helped us an awful lot, but it's our baby now."

I agreed but deep down I knew I would not let this go.

Paddy and Simon were busy taking statements, including one from me, but I was left until last, so I took the opportunity to ring Dennis and tell him what had happened.

Typically he threw a wobbler. "Even with my trade discount, you're looking at two and a half ton. What with the front window at home and now two windows on your heap of junk, you'll be pushing the glass manufacturer's share price up. Stay put, I'll come and get you. Oh, and before you moan, I'll be in the wrecker cos I'll have to tow the Fiat back."

I didn't get chance to talk further because Dennis cut the call off and at the same time, Paddy called me to give him a statement. I kept it brief and factual, and when I was through, he had me sign it.

"Your version agrees with Springer's. What threw him over the top was you accusing him of murdering Becky Walmer."

"He did," I insisted.

"I think so too, but we're wrong, Chrissy." Paddy was only usually that definite when he knew something I didn't. "He has a cast iron alibi."

"His wife, you mean? She's lying. She was in the maternity ward at The Cottage that night."

"I'm not talking about his wife. He was with Nancy Farmer all night at her place, and she swears he never left her bed."

I had to wonder how many shocks my system could stand in one morning.

"If we can't break her, cancel his alibi, we've nothing on him," Paddy was saying. "We could do him for criminal damage to your car, but this guy isn't stupid. He's ready to apologise to you and he's agreed to make restitution. Whatever the cost of replacing your windscreen and the driver's window, he'll pay."

"Dennis is on his way with the wrecker. I'll tell him to bill Springer's."

"Good. Now you need to back off and let this go, girl. You've done a good job. You proved Prater couldn't have done it, you've got him out of the nick and he'll be due a fair slice of compo. Leave the rest of it to us."

223

"While Springer senior gets away with murder?"

"Come on, lass. You were one of us. You know the score. We can't win them all."

"Yes, but what about Springer's son? Robbie?"

"We have him and his mate bang to rights for hitting Teddy Anguage and trying it on with Dennis. If they killed Frank Penning, they'll have left traces and forensic will guide us on that. We're also checking with immigration to see if they hopped on a plane to Malaga a few days ago to deal with Pete Kitson. Denby has admitted taking one of Prater's jumpers and handing it over to Kitson, but he doesn't know who was behind it all."

"You mean he says he doesn't know."

"Whatever. And to press, we can't break him either… and before you even think about it, you're not going to have a go at him."

"It never crossed my mind. Paddy, I don't care what Springer says, or what Nancy Farmer tells you, it was him who murdered Becky. I'm sure of it. You should have seen the way he lost it with me earlier."

"I said, I'm with you, but unless we can break her or dig up something out of Kitson's history or Penning's we'll never know. Look at it this way, Chrissy. Something or someone brought those two to Haxford that morning when me and Linda Risley got there, and that same someone or something persuaded them to plant the thread from Jacko's jumper." Paddy shrugged. "If it turns out that they hadn't had a payoff from Springer, then it had to be one of them."

"I don't believe it, but if it was, my money

224

would be on Kitson... all right, all right, I know, you thought the sun shone out of his Y-fronts but so did he; literally. He was well known for trying to bed every woman at Haxford station. He even tried it on with Mandy and me..." I realised how gross that might sound so I hastened on. "Individually and years apart, and it didn't get him anywhere. And according to everyone I've spoken to, Becky Walmer wasn't shy about leaping on any man."

Paddy shook his head. "Give me some proof. Give me some evidence, even, and I'll look at it. Until then, let it go."

I came out of the office in a subdued mood, to find Dennis, hands on hips, the wrecker parked nearby, and he was looking over the damage to the Diablo. He shook his head sadly as I joined him.

"It's a right flaming mess. And do you know how much this'll cost?"

"Nothing, Mr Capper." We both looked round at the sound of Brian Springer's voice. "If you send me the bill, I'll cover the cost of any repairs, and if you, Mrs Capper, need to hire a vehicle for the time being, then I'll stand the cost of that, too."

I wanted nothing from this man but payment for the damage to my car. "I'll borrow Dennis's car. He won't mind, will you Dennis?"

"Yeah, but—"

"You see." I gave Springer a cynical smile. "As a husband, Dennis knows how to take care of his wife."

If I expected him to pick up on me, he let me down. "Please accept my apologies for what happened. I was out of control after you accused me of killing that poor girl."

"It seems I owe you an apology on the same score, Mr Springer." I almost choked on the words. "What I can't understand is your son's actions."

"Me neither," he admitted, "but I suspect he was trying to protect his mother. I'm not saying Pauline had anything to do with Becky's murder. She was actually at home that night, and not at Jumping Jacks nor in the maternity unit of The Cottage. Victoria, our daughter, was actually born a few days earlier. But Pauline was still post-natal, and she had difficulty in moving around. You're a mother. I'm sure you know what I'm talking about."

I did. I was housebound for several days after a difficult labour with Ingrid.

A thin smile spread across Springer's face. "Mother always said I should never have married anyone from the Langdon family. New money, you see. Not like the Springer's. And they're Low Church. Didn't meet with Mam's approval on any front. She was wrong, of course. Mother, I mean. Pauline has been the absolute best of wives."

I don't think he realised just how important his words were to me, but I covered it by saying, "No offence, Mr Springer, but your reputation would argue with your final words. I'll bid you good day."

The thin smile came back. "And I can't be held responsible for what other people think of me. Good day to you, Mrs Capper."

With him gone, I focussed on Dennis. "I don't—"

"Listen, Chrissy, I don't really want you driving the Marina."

226

"Shut your mouth and open your ears, Dennis, I was about to say I don't want to run around in that piece of old rubbish. I only said that to get rid of him."

"My Marina is not a piece of old rubbish." He gestured at the Diablo. "This is, but not my Marina."

"That's a matter of opinion. Do you have anything else at the workshop I can borrow until you get the Diablo repaired?"

He stroked his chin. "Well, we've got an old Renault Clio which we were gonna sell. It's got a full MOT and stuff."

My mood lifted. "Ooh. Like the one I had before we got the Diablo?"

"Pretty much, but a good few years older."

"Well, why don't you let me have that... permanently?"

"Yeah, but like I say, we were gonna sell it."

"Sell the Diablo instead." He was not convinced. "Dennis, you keep saying that the Diablo is too big for us now that you don't need the wheelchair and stuff."

"You can borrow it and I'll see what the others have to say about a straight swap."

I had to wait around while he hooked the Diablo onto a piece of apparatus called an A-frame, and then lifted the front end so that wrecker could tow it. And then he had to help me into the wrecker which I would call a large lorry but which Dennis described as medium sized, and then we were on our way.

"If it were anyone but you, I could have had them sit in and steer the Diablo on a rigid tow, but you'd only moan you were cold."

I hadn't the foggiest idea what he was talking about, but the lorry, I decided, was just as cold and several magnitudes more uncomfortable than the Diablo. Still and all, fifteen minutes later, we stopped outside Haxford Fixers' premises, and after a brief chat with the boys, I climbed behind the wheel of the silver-grey Renault and drove off towards Haxford.

It was like coming home. Before the Diablo, I'd had my nearly new Clio for a good few years, and although this was older, the controls were similar. It needed a good valet (Tony Wharrier would do it for me) and there were some fiddly bits which could do with mending. The glove type thing that fits round the gear lever had come away, for example, and I had a dashboard light warning me that one of the doors was not properly shut. They all were, so I assumed it to be a minor electrical glitch. I was sure Lester would deal with that for me.

I had neither the time nor patience to savour the pleasure of driving it. I was in a lot of a hurry. Brian Springer had let slip one tiny piece of information and I needed to act on it right away. I knew for sure now who murdered Becky Walmer and I knew why.

I was Christine Capper, blogger, vlogger, private eye, radio personality, afraid of no one, not even the high and mighty James Langdon, and before long, he would be on his knees begging me to forget our previous disagreement, putting the torn contract back together with Sellotape and pleading with me to carry on as one of the stars of Radio Haxford. And it wouldn't do him one ha'pporth of good. Before the day was out, he would be on his way to jail… for life.

This was all very well in theory, but when I got to the upper gallery of the market hall, I hit first obstacle; the pig-headed security man guarding the studio door.

"I have a meeting with Mr Langdon."

"Not according to my schedule, you don't. You're only allowed in here on Tuesday mornings and it's Friday."

"He doesn't know about the meeting, but he will want to see me."

"Not interested. Now do us both a favour, Mrs C, and—"

"Get Eric Reitman out here."

"Huh?"

"You heard. Shout Eric Reitman. He'll let me in." The last thing he wanted to do was speak to Eric, but I stood my ground. "Get him out here. Now."

He began talking into his radio and I backed off, leaned on the balustrade and looked out over the market hall. This was one of my favourite places. I loved the atmosphere, the friendliness of the traders, digging out the bargains, and when my eye fell upon Terry's Tea Bar, I could almost taste the gastronomic delight of his tea and teacakes.

"Chrissy, what's going on?"

I turned to find Eric behind me and I aimed a thumb at the security man. "I need to speak to Langdon, and this idiot won't let me in."

"I'm doing my job, missus, and I'm not an idiot."

"That last is debatable," I said and confronted Eric. "To be fair to Langdon, I can't tell you what's going on, but it's vital that I see him."

"I doubt that he'll give you the time of day. I mean, if you were willing to climb down, I could negotiate on your behalf, but…"

I didn't wait for any more excuses. I barged past them and into the studio, Eric and the security guard hot on my tail. To a raft of amazed stares from the crew (even Reggie gaped through the glass screen of his broadcast studio) I marched straight between the lines of desks, pushed my way through the connecting door, and hurried up the stairs to the top floor. Once there, I didn't pause. Despite the attempts of his PA to stop me, I strode straight into Langdon's office. It was a sign of the man's total control that no one, not even the PA, followed me, and I slammed the door behind me.

Chapter Twenty-One

Langdon was on the phone, and the moment I appeared, he made his excuses, ended the call and put the receiver down. Leaning forward, resting on his forearms, he aimed a steady finger at the way out. "There's the door. Close it as you leave."

I ignored him, and sat down.

"Get... Out." The pause was deliberate, designed to underline his increasing anger. Once again I ignored him.

"Are you deaf or just plain stupid?"

Springer asked the same question in a roundabout way, and I didn't back away from him. I wasn't backing away now.

"The police arrested Brian Springer's boy last night. He's guilty of the murder of former Detective Sergeant Frank Penning, and possibly that of DCI Peter Kitson. Everything is out of my hands now, it's all a police matter and I reckon they'll be here within the hour. The minute Robbie Springer tells them who paid him to kill those two retired cops."

On receiving the news, his face paled a little. "All that has nothing to do with—"

I cut him off. "What concerns me isn't the outcome of those inquiries. Jack Prater will be released, he will pick up a huge amount of compensation, but of course, that won't give him back the twenty years he lost in prison, and I think he'll be a very angry man, angry enough to go looking for all those people who knew and covered up the real killer. And you, Langdon, are likely to be right at the top of his list."

"You should be careful what you're saying. My lawyers—"

I cut him off for the second time. "I got into a bit of a spat with Brian Springer this morning. The police had to come and sort it out. It all ended fairly amicably but he passed an innocent little comment. I don't think he even realised what he was saying. Quote, 'Mother always said I should never have married anyone from the Langdon family', unquote. Curious coincidence, don't you think? Pauline Springer, née Langdon. The same surname as you. New money and Low Church. That's how he described your family." His colour drained further and I pressed home my attack. "You tried to shut me up, you pile of dog muck; tore my contract to shreds and for what? To cover up your strangling Becky Walmer. And your daughter, Pauline Springer, knew, didn't she? Her and her womanising husband. You sent the threats to me, and you had those idiots smash my front window. You sent Robbie and his pal after Kitson, Penning, and my husband. Yes, and they came a cropper didn't they? Bit off more than they could chew when they met Dennis and his mates. Well, now it's your turn."

I always considered myself a sympathetic woman, but I took a perverse delight in the look of utter defeat on his face. I had no pity for him. If he was on the floor begging, I would have trodden him into the carpet.

"If you'll allow me to correct you, Mrs Capper, you have one or two things wrong."

Suddenly, I was Mrs Capper. Suddenly he was treating me with some respect. Just as he should. Who did he think he was dealing with? I didn't want to hear anything he had to say, but I nevertheless gave some ground. "I'm listening."

"First, I did not murder Rebecca Walmer. I couldn't. I was in London at an awards ceremony with your friend, Reitman. Had anyone asked, I would have proved it at the time, but no one did ask because no one connected me to that appalling crime. Therefore, I never had to confirm my whereabouts"

He was in London? Jack Prater was in London? Was everyone in London that Easter? How could I get it so wrong so many times in one morning?

"Second," he went on, "Pauline Springer is not my daughter. She's my niece. Did I know about Brian's involvement with this young woman? Yes, I did, but it was a peripheral issue. The police did question Brian, and dismissed him from their enquiries. Pauline was just out of hospital and housebound with a new baby, so as far as I was concerned, neither of them had anything to do with Rebecca's death. And gossip had it that everyone involved in that case knew who really killed her."

Jack Prater's words came back to me. *He (Kitson) knew who did that girl. So did I. So did everyone.*

Everyone but me, that is. I'd accused so many

233

people, including the man opposite that I wasn't sure who I was, let alone who killed Becky.

Langdon hadn't finished. "Finally, young Robbie, my great nephew is as big an idiot as his father, but I didn't send him and his friend after you, your husband, or Frank Penning, but if they did it – and I'm not sure of that, either – and the police have them, then good. They should be punished."

I wasn't sure whether or not I believed him, but on balance, I felt he was telling the truth. His attitude had receded. He was no longer the pushy, 'I'm in charge and you'll do as I say' individual I'd met on the previous occasion, but talking in normal, reasonable tones, and that was enough to persuade me that he was being absolutely honest, or something very close to it. A bit like me telling Dennis that I'd only spent twenty pounds on cosmetics when it was closer to thirty.

I was in control of proceedings, and I wasn't going to let him get off that easily. "Right now, Mr Langdon, I'm more concerned with that business of you tearing up my contract? What kind of game were you playing?"

He didn't answer right away. He half turned in his chair, to gaze through the panoramic windows at the rooftops of Haxford town centre. When he turned back there was an air of – I don't know – reflective calm about him. "You've been married a long time, you have children, and according to Reitman, you were in Cambridge a little while ago, for the wedding of your brother's daughter."

"I don't see the relevance."

"I'm coming to it. Family is important to you, is

it, Mrs Capper?"

Relevant or otherwise, the question caused me to stop and think. For me, family had always been the most important factor in my life. Dennis and I never had to make too many sacrifices for Simon or Ingrid, but when called upon to do so, we did. My children would take over the mantle when Dennis and I entered our dotage. As they made their way in the world, so my focus had switched to the next generation, darling Bethany, the hyperactive, excitable little girl I indulged so shamelessly.

"Yes. Family is important to me."

"To me too," Langdon said. "I wasn't born to money or power, you know. Everything I have, including my position as controller of Radio Haxford, I've worked for." He laughed. "New money. Isn't that what Brian said? Well, maybe that's true, but I never lost sight of the importance of family. My brother, my sister, my children, my siblings' children. They matter to me. Each and every one of them. I was at their wedding, you know. Brian and Pauline's, and I was so pleased, proud to see that woman, whom I'd known ever since she was a little girl, dressed in white, marrying the man she loved."

Another brief silence fell upon the room.

"Trouble is, that man was – is – feckless. A gadabout. I don't know how many different women he was bedding, even after he and Pauline were married. He's been involved with that PA of his, that Nancy Farmer for years, and of course, he had taken Rebecca Walmer to bed more than once." A thin, cynical smile spread across his lips. "You can't

235

choose your children's partners, can you? And you certainly can't choose your niece's partner. I guessed that Pauline must have suffered thanks to his inability to keep his pants on, yet she stayed with him because he was a good provider and because she loves him."

Yet another brief silence. At that point, I could see no reason for me to prompt him or to intervene, so I maintained my passive position.

"I remember the murder of that poor young woman. It was all over the news even in the capital. She was born of the same mould as Brian Springer. Anything in trousers in her case, but however good or bad she was, she didn't deserve that. I also knew she worked for Brian, as I've just hinted when I said he had his way with her. I didn't believe for one moment that Brian or Pauline had anything to do with her death, and in any case, inside forty-eight hours, the police had Prater for the crime. Open and shut case, cut and dried, end of story.... Except that it wasn't."

At last, I could see where he was going. "You mean I opened up a can of worms."

"Correct." A note of pleading came into his voice. "Twenty years ago, I knew nothing other than Brian had slept with the girl. He can be bad tempered when he wants, Brian, but I believed that he would stop short of murder."

It crossed my mind that Langdon was not sat in my car earlier with Brian Springer threatening to shuffle me off my mortal coil otherwise, he might revise his opinion of his niece's husband.

I said nothing but carried on listening.

"As far as I was concerned, it was history until you started asking questions. Believe me, I was thinking of Pauline. I didn't want her to be hurt, to have all those memories of Brian's infidelity brought up." He forced a little smile. "As it turned out, circumstances worked in my favour. I said, I didn't get where I am today without a lot of hard work and some smart manoeuvring. Your mystery hour is, frankly, rubbish. The ratings are garbage. Even without the Prater case, that programme was doomed, and I used that in an effort to bring you to heel. Your prison visit, the police turning up here to arrest Reitman, it all slotted nicely into the disrepute clause in your contract. It was just perfect. So I insisted you drop it on pain of tearing up your contract."

"And did you really think you'd get away with it?"

"I'm used to getting what I want." He took a deep breath and let it out as a long sigh. "What threw me was your stubbornness. I said, I always get my own way. If I dragged Reggie Monk in here, ordered him to take a shower and see a dentist on pain of excommunication, he would be on his knees, begging me to give him a chance. You're different. You wouldn't give in. Even after I tore up the contract, which was a photocopy by the way, you refused to back off." A soft, cynical chuckle this time. "I can't recall ever coming across that kind of resistance. Reitman has been in here almost every day, begging me to reconsider on your behalf. Obviously, I couldn't back down, and the feedback I got from him told me that you were not willing to

237

back down either."

"Unstoppable force meeting the immovable object," I suggested.

"Precisely," he agree. "And all so pointless. If you're right about Robbie's antics, the history will come out in open court, and Pauline will suffer the kind of pain I always wanted to spare her. Beyond that, you and I are still at loggerheads, so the entire exercise was a waste of adrenalin from my point of view. However, no matter what agreement you and I can come to right now, I don't believe that Brian or Pauline had anything to do with the murder of Rebecca Walmer."

If I were to be honest with myself, I would admit that I still didn't like the man, and although I might not agree with him about his niece's husband, his words rang loud bells, reverberating through my entire being. Would I fight for Simon, Ingrid, Naomi, Bethany, even Stephen, and his daughter, Jocelyn? Too right I would.

This time the silence fell upon me while I tried to work out whether or not he was telling the truth. Eventually, I decided I believed him.

I cleared my throat. A theatrical preamble before speaking. "As I said when I first came in, the police may want to speak to you, and given the background to the case, the late DCI Kitson and Sergeant Penning's possible conspiracy to cover up the crime, it may be that the IOPC will want a word with you, too. In either case, when it's all over, if I were in your position, I would make a public statement on the matter. As far as I'm concerned, you're guilty of nothing but a misjudgement based on family loyalty. I don't think there's any need for me to hassle you any further, Mr Langdon. And please accept my apologies for bursting in the way I did this morning."

"Apology accepted, and I hope you will accept my apologies for the whole mess."

We shook hands and I prepared to leave, but he stayed me.

"Not so fast. You and I, Christine – you don't mind if I call you Christine, do you – have to decide where we go from here. With regard to Radio Haxford, that is."

When I first confronted him it was with the intention of a) bringing him before the police, and b) securing the payoff for the eighteen months my contract still had to run.

I shrugged. "If Radio Haxford are willing to pay me any outstanding fees on my contract, we can leave it at that."

He wagged a finger at me and I detected the return of forceful control. "Oh no. You don't get out of it that easily. I do listen to Reitman, you know, and he assures me that you are a natural for radio. He's always insisted upon it ever since you were persuaded to take on the agony aunt spot. The mystery hour is a dead duck. Let's be clear on that. But that doesn't mean to say that Christine Capper is finished with Radio Haxford, and I've had an idea. Let me run it past you."

Again I shrugged, but unwilling to give anything away, I remained guarded. "I'm listening." Hadn't I said that once?

"This whole sorry mess has taught me one thing

about you. You are an expert at getting information from people. So, here's what I'm thinking—"

A point occurred to me and I interrupted. "One moment." When he fell silent, I went on. "You say everyone knows who murdered that young woman. I don't, so tell me. Who was it?"

He laughed. "You're the detective. Work it out. Why would a smart cop like Kitson drag an idiot like Brian Springer into the mess? Why not pin it on Brian? It would have been just as easy as landing it at Jack Prater's door. Think about it, Christine, and you'll see that the answer is obvious."

Chapter Twenty-Two

There's a small, popular parking area just past the peak of the hill at Moor Top, not far from Allbrook Farm, and from there, the view is spectacular. You can see the whole of Haxford in the valley below, and spread all around on the plateau, was the vast, near-wilderness that was the moors. To the east, bathed in afternoon sunlight, was the giant, concrete tower of Emley Moor TV transmitter with its new, skeletal, metal partner stood alongside. To the west, looking towards Manchester and north Derbyshire, was the tall, thin mast of the Holme Moss transmitter. They were the towers from where we got our TV and mobile phone signals. Scattered at key points on the crests of various hills, were boosters, designed to ensure the signals were beamed down to our TV sets, mobile phones, and radios. As a network, they ensured that Haxford kept in touch with the rest of the world.

After leaving the studio, I popped home, checked on Cappy the Cat, then paid a quick visit to Hazel McQuarrie next door, and told her where I would be for the next hour or two.

"I have some serious thinking to do, Hazel, and I need something that will infuse and invigorate me. And I don't mean booze."

"Shame," Hazel replied. "When I need an infusion, I've always found alcohol to be the best."

Then I drove up to Moor Top Viewpoint, turned the car round to face Haxford, and shut down the engine. From now (early May) throughout the summer, this place would be busy. There would be a little caravan where the proprietor sold tea, coffee, soft drinks and snacks. But it was still slightly too early in the year for visitors or the snack van. Either that or everyone was staying at home, getting ready to watch the coronation. No matter, I was totally alone on this beautiful, spring afternoon. Beautiful, calming, but with a fresh breeze sweeping across the moors. When it came to the need for inspiration and contemplation, there was nothing finer than the solitude of Moor Top Viewpoint.

The interlude with Langdon ended amicably, and after listening to his idea, the Christine Capper Interview was already on the drawing board. It would be recorded, not live, and sometimes those interviews would take place in my conservatory (and I would need better quality teabags for my guests than I supplied for the crew). However, just as often, I would be visiting the interviewee's home, office, or wherever. We could possibly deal with the interview in public places like the Barncroft Memorial Park or the grounds of the Haxford Cottage Hospital. Wherever the guest wanted. My career in radio, in tatters just a few days ago, was assured.

Assuming the researchers could find enough people willing to talk on radio, it would become a weekly programme, but at the outset, we were concentrating on one hour per fortnight. The contract, which I'd signed in Langdon's presence and which was witnessed by his PA, paid me the same as the mystery hour and Lost Friends, but both those programmes were to be consigned to the dustbin of the tried, tested, and best forgotten. True, Lost Friends would continue, but only as a fifteen-minute slot during Reggie Monk's Thursday morning programme and it would be delivered by someone other than me (I hadn't been told who and frankly, I didn't care).

With the formal business out of the way, Langdon called Eric to his office and we went through the idea together. As programme director and producer, it would be his task to see that the Christine Capper Interview came to fruition. Half an hour later, I came away with Eric as a friend again.

It would be stretching a point to say that I liked Langdon, but he was right about one thing. When it came to talking with people, I had ways and means of teasing out answers to difficult questions, and if I was serious about a career – albeit part-time – in radio, then the Christine Capper Interview was the logical move for me. As long as I remained challenging but neutral, and provided there were enough people willing to be interviewed, I could foresee a long run of success.

Looking back on the day from a broader angle, the Prater case led me to another firm conclusion. Ever since the Leach affair the previous August, I had hesitated, dithered, wavered on whether or not to keep my PI licence. Now I knew the answer. I was simply too good to let it go. Didn't I solve the problem at Christmas Manor, wasn't I instrumental in cracking the Allbrook/Keogh case, didn't I pinpoint the truth at Gaven hall, and hadn't I just proved Jack Prater's innocence? It would be a waste of my talents if I gave it up.

If there was a downside, I hadn't cracked the case of Becky Walmer's murder, but when I thought about Langdon's final words, it did indeed become obvious. A call to Paddy confirmed it. Most of Haxford thought that Pete Kitson murdered that poor girl. The theory was, Kitson took her to bed (let's face it, that was his reputation with women) and she demanded a payoff on pain of exposing him to his bosses, whereupon he shut her up for keeps.

I didn't buy it. I still believed it was Brian Springer, but as Paddy said, without some kind of evidence, we would probably never know.

With my visit to the Radio Haxford studio, all my problems (bar one) were suddenly solved. Dennis was the odd man out, but he was easy. A little frank talking and we would go back to what we always had been: a solid partnership, a couple who had started with love, which over the years turned to undying affection and unbreakable bonds.

I looked down on the town, picking out the highlights. The cottage hospital, the memorial park, St Asaph's church, and huddled in the town centre, the market hall, with Radio Haxford's transmission mast on the roof, the library where my good friend, Kim Aspinall and her man, Alden Upley held court. There was Batley Road Estate, home of the Prater clan, and swinging to the other side of town, there stood The Woolcombers where Linda's police career came to a violent end. Turning my head back to the right, I could see Haxford Mill, and on the side closest to me, clearly visible, Haxford Fixers' wrecker, the tow truck that Dennis and his partners made so much use of. Even without binoculars and x-ray vision, I knew that in that workshop, he and his pals would be engrossed in their work, and in the background, Radio Haxford would be entertaining them.

This was where I belonged. I was a born and bred Haxforder, I loved Haxford. A blot on the landscape, some commentators called the town, an eyesore fit only for erasure from the pages of Ordnance Survey maps. Nonsense. I was part of Haxford and Haxford was a part of me. I could never imagine any future that did not encompass this little mill town and could not envisage a Yorkshire where Haxford did not exist.

How fitting then, that I would still be one of the voices of Radio Haxford. Never mind Radio Leeds, Radio Sheffield or any of the other local-ish stations, I was one of those people who would keep Haxford in the forefront of local minds, push the town, help our community prosper, let the country know that we were there, that Haxford mattered, that the people of Haxford mattered.

I don't know how long I sat there wallowing in this absurd vision of our little town as the centre of the universe, but I had to run the engine a couple of times to draw heat into the Clio's cockpit.

Then I saw a dirty, dark blue van crest the hill, and accelerate in my direction. I wanted to be alone and I prayed it was a vet, hurtling on his way to an emergency at one of the outlying farms, but I knew it wasn't. All our vets ran flashy, fancy new cars. Cappy the Cat's vet must have been an outstanding success considering the big Audi he ran around in. Actually, he didn't need to be a rampant success. When I thought about the thirty pounds he'd charged for ten minutes work and few claw marks, I reckon his fees were enough to support two big Audis.

As it drew near, I realised it was the Haxford Fixers van. Dennis or Greg or Tony, I guessed, on the way to a breakdown.

Yet again, I was wrong. Not about the identity of the van, but its destination. It was Dennis and he was on his way to me.

He slewed the van into the parking area, brought it to a slurring halt alongside the Renault, and barely pausing to switch the engine off, leapt out and jumped into the Clio's passenger seat.

"What are you doing out here, Chrissy?"

"Taking a break." The obvious question occurred to me. "How did you know I was here?"

"Mandy rang our place, asked if we knew where you were. They need another statement from you or summat. I tried your phone but it's switched off, so I rang old Ma Mcq and she told me you'd come up here to sink some booze. I thought I'd better come looking for you. I didn't want you doing owt stupid while you're full of ale."

I smiled. "Hazel's got a one-track mind and it leads to the bar not the bed. I never mentioned alcohol."

"It still don't explain why you're here. Is it that

246

Prater business?"

"No. That's sorted, Dennis, and I did it. I didn't actually find out who killed young Becky, but I did prove that Jack Prater was innocent all along."

He grunted. "You usually do get 'em sorted. So what is it that's bothering you, then? That business about you on the wireless?"

"No. I sorted that out, too."

"They're gonna pay you up?" His eyes lit up and I could almost see the pound signs reflected in them

"Not quite, but I will get my money. I've got a new programme. The Christine Capper Interview. It starts later this month." His face fell. "So what's wrong with that, Dennis?"

"Nowt."

"You mean you were hoping they'd just pay me off and let go."

"Aye. Summat like that."

"It's me, Dennis. That's what I am. A private eye and a radio presenter."

"No. You're my missus. You're Chrissy."

It was the kind of comment that would spark a row, but somehow I didn't think Dennis meant it like that. My reply reflected the inner calm I had felt a few moments back. "What are you talking about?"

He didn't answer right away. Instead he gazed at the surrounding landscape, but in contrast to the way I had admired it, I guessed he was trying to find a way of putting his thoughts into words.

"There was this bloke up in Scotland or somewhere who won the lottery big style. Millions, he collected, and he said he was the luckiest bloke alive. He was wrong. I'm the luckiest bloke in this world cos you picked me as your old man."

This was amazing. In almost thirty years, I'd never heard Dennis say anything close to this. And he wasn't finished.

"Y'see, it's happen me that's to blame, cos I don't make such a big deal about it, but the fact is, I need you, Chrissy. Left on me own, I'm hopeless. Oh, I can listen to a motor and tell you what's wrong with it. I can look at any old car and give you a list of its tech specs. But that's work, that's what I do. When it comes to other stuff, I have to have you to put me right. If I had to do the shopping I'd come home with a loaf of bread and a sack of spuds and live on nowt but chip butties. I'd have to buy me dinners at the Snacky or somewhere. I'd end up like Grimy, only instead of living in the bar of the Sump Hole, I'd be dossing in the workshop. I bring the money in, cos that's what I'm good for, and I'm not saying you don't earn your share, but you do a lot more than just bringing in a few bob. You make sure it gets spent where it should. That's it, lass. That's what you are. An organiser. You get us organised because I can't."

I was still stunned by his admissions, but I never got the chance to say a word as he went on.

"Think about last year when them two scrotes gave me a good hiding. You were the one who really paid for that cos I was out of it most of the time. Helpless. You had to do everything; minding the house, doing your bits and pieces of work, the shopping, everything, including changing them frilly knickers when I messed meself. Where would

248

I have been if you hadn't been there?"

The 'frilly knickers' he was talking about were incontinence pants and as he mentioned them I remembered the near-parental care I had to deliver. It was like dealing with a newborn baby only he was more difficult to manhandle.

I picked up on his final point. "But I was there, Dennis. I'm always there."

"I know you were, and I know you're always there and that means I don't have to worry cos I know you'll look after me which means I can get on with the stuff I know best. Motors. You put me right when I'm wrong, and let's face, I'm wrong more'n I'm right, aren't I? You make sure I have enough clobber in the wardrobe so when we have to go somewhere like your Stephen's lass's wedding, I look like I'm supposed to instead of a scruff. And you deal with a ton of other stuff that I can't because aside from mending cars, I'm useless."

While he was saying all this, he continued to stare at our surroundings. Now he turned to face me.

"But you've changed, Chrissy. Ever since that shindig at the manor last Christmas, it's like Radio Haxford and Reitman come first, second, and last. You've been getting out of your pram over other people and the bits and pieces you've been poking your nose into. Like Allbrook, like Norrell in Cambridge, and now Prater. I'm not saying you were wrong. You weren't. But it's like they were taking over our lives."

I smiled. "Don't forget my affair with Eric Reitman."

He gave me a small smile too. "That's only me

being daft. We've been together too long, lass, for me not to know. If you were carrying on with someone else, even a numpty like me would twig." The smile faded. "It's norrupter me to say what you can and can't do, but you're getting too involved. Crikey, this last week you've been sulking in the conservatory of a night so we don't even sit down and watch the telly together no more."

"I've not been sulking, I've been thinking, and I don't want to watch some nerd yakking about high performance cars, or watching a couple of anoraks rebuilding a classic car."

A solid observation but Dennis had a ready answer. "I only watch them cos I'm on me own. If you were there we'd have proper telly on." His features became even more serious. "I'm not clever with words, Chrissy. You know that, so I might have it all wrong, but I feel like we're falling apart and I don't want that. I don't want to lose you."

And with that, I knew why we had been so solid for that last three decades. I took his hand and immediately wished I hadn't. His hands were covered in grime and now, so was mine.

"I've had a confusing week and a few days, Dennis, and most of what you're saying has already come home to me. You're right. I have been too engrossed in the things I'm investigating. You're right. I do need to learn to switch off of a night. I'll do it and you don't have to worry. We're not drifting apart. The big difference between us is that I really will get on with it, put it right, whereas you still won't be able to cook anything other than chips, and even then, you'll set fire to the wallpaper."

Epilogue

That was as far as I went with the case but it's not quite the whole story.

About a month after the magnificent spectacle of King Charles III coronation, Paddy received a document from Pete Kitson's widow. She'd been sorting out the routine detritus of a sudden death, getting ready to move back to the UK, when she turned it up. It was a computerised journal and when she read it, she copied it to a CD and sent it to Haxford station.

On the night of Becky Walmer's murder, Brian Springer contacted Kitson, a golfing buddy, and told him what had happened. As I suggested at Springer's on that final Friday morning, Springer tried his luck at Jumping Jacks, Becky refused unless he made arrangements to put her up in her own place and effectively become his mistress. If he turned her down, she would tell Pauline about the number of times he had bedded Nancy Farmer and those times Becky and he had shared the back seat of his car.

In a furious temper, he got to her home before her, forced his way in, killed the dog and when she arrived, he strangled her.

In a panic, he asked Kitson to get him off the

hook. The price, fifty thousand. Kitson would get thirty, Penning the other twenty. It seemed that both Kitson and Penning felt they owed Prater for the way he had wriggled out of some burglary charge a couple of years previously, so they decided upon him as the fall guy, and gave Springer instructions to see Elaine Anguage to secure an item of clothing... any item of clothing from which they could take the incriminating thread. Kitson and Penning were not only at the Walmers' place before Paddy and Linda; they were there all night, setting up the frame, and of course it was one of them who posed as the anonymous neighbour to raise the alarm with a call to the police.

Kitson wrote it all down because he didn't entirely trust Springer and in the event, of course, he was right.

When Paddy and Mandy confronted Springer with the damning account, he broke down and confessed. He also admitted to sending his son and friend to Spain to deal with Kitson, then sicked them onto Penning, and me, and when they couldn't get to me, he sent them to deal with Dennis. Both the Springers, Brian and Robbie, and Robbie's pal would be spending a long time in prison.

Before that, however, Jack Prater was released in the middle of May in a blaze of media attention and it was estimated that his compensation would be on par with a lottery win. Within a month of his release, he was caught stealing a bag of tomatoes from CutCost. When he appeared in court, he was fined, notwithstanding his claim that he was simply making sure he hadn't lost any of his old skills. The last we heard, he, Elaine, and their offspring were considering a move to the south coast.

I learned so much during that unsettled fortnight. Unlike Jacko, I really did reaffirm my skills as a private eye, I learned that I had new-found confidence to tackle biggies like James Langdon, but I also learned that I was not the be-all and end-all to either private investigation or local radio. I had to know when to step back.

There was something else, something far more important. I discovered just how much I meant to Dennis. I learned that I was a good woman married to a good man. I had always known it, yet it took that little interlude at Moor Top Viewpoint to remind me of it. My work as a private eye would go on, my radio spots would go on, but most important, one thing that (in my mind) had never been in doubt, would also go on: Dennis and me.

And that's it for this edition of Christine Capper's Comings & Goings. Stop by again next week for more happenings in and around Haxford.

THE END

THANK YOU FOR READING. I HOPE YOU HAVE ENJOYED THIS BOOK. WOULD YOU BE KIND ENOUGH TO LEAVE A RATING OR REVIEW ON AMAZON?

The Author

David W Robinson retired from the rat race after the other rats objected to his participation, and he now lives with his long-suffering wife in sight of the Pennine Moors outside Manchester.

Best known as the creator of the light-hearted and ever-popular **Sanford 3rd Age Club Mysteries**, and in the same vein, **Mrs Capper's Casebook**. He also produces darker, more psychological crime thrillers as in the **Feyer & Drake** thrillers and occasional standalone titles.

He, produces his own videos, and can frequently be heard grumbling against the world on Facebook at https://www.facebook.com/davidrobinsonwriter/

and has a YouTube channel at https://www.youtube.com/user/Dwrob96/videos.
For more information you can track him down at www.dwrob.com and if you want to sign up to my newsletter and pick up a #FREE book or two, you can find all the details at https://dwrob.com/readers-club/

By the same Author
Mrs Capper's Casebook

Christine Capper is a solid, down to earth Yorkshire lass, witty, plain spoken, but with an innate sense of inquiry (all right, then, she's nosy). She passes her days in the West Yorkshire town of Haxford looking after her long-suffering husband, Dennis, a man with an obsession for all things automotive, and putting him right when he goes wrong, which is more often than not. She takes care of their pet, Cappy the Cat, a feline with attitude, dotes on her granddaughter Bethany, and is openly proud of her son, Simon, now Acting Detective Constable Capper of the Haxford force.

A former police officer, she's Haxford's only trained and licenced private investigator. She's choosy about the cases she takes on but appears destined to be dragged into more serious affairs, during which she passes on her findings to her friend, Detective Sergeant Mandy Hiscoe and

Mandy's immediate boss, DI Paddy Quinn, a man who is quite open about his dislike for private eyes.

A series of light-hearted mysteries, laced with Yorkshire grit and wit, Mrs Capper's Casebooks are exclusive to Amazon available for the Kindle and in paperback.

You can find them at:
https://mybook.to/cappseries

The Sanford 3rd Age Club Mysteries

These titles are published and managed by Darkstroke Books

A decade on from their debut, there are 26 volumes (soon to be 27) and a special in the Sanford 3rd Age Club Mystery series.

We follow the travels and trials of amateur sleuth Joe Murray and his two best friends, Sheila Riley and Brenda Jump. The short, irascible Joe, proprietor of The Lazy Luncheonette in Sanford, West Yorkshire, jollied along by the bubbly Brenda and Sheila, but only his friends, but also his employees, all three leading lights in the Sanford 3rd Age Club (STAC for short). And it seems that wherever they go on their outings on holidays in the company of the born-again teenagers of the 3rd Age Club, they bump into… MURDER.

A major series of whodunits marinated in Yorkshire

humour, they are exclusive to Amazon and you can find them at: **https://mybook.to/stac**

Other Works

I also turn out darker works such as The Anagramist and The Frame with Chief Inspector Samantha Feyer and civilian consultant Wesley Drake, and the standalone The Cutter.

For details visit https://dwrob.com/the-dark/

Free Books

Like what you've seen so far? Why to subscribe to my newsletter? I guaranteed that you will not be inundated with emails, and your address will never be sold on. Once you sign up, you will receive details of to one but TWO free novellas.

For more information visit
https://dwrob.com/readers-club/

Printed in Great Britain
by Amazon